ALSO BY TIM SANDLIN

Sex and Sunsets

Western Swing

Skipped Parts

Sorrow Floats

Social Blunders

Lydia

Honey Don't

Rowdy in Paris

Jimi Hendrix Turns Eighty

The Fable of Bing

The Pyms: Unauthorized Tales of Jackson Hole

SOMEWHAT TRUE TALES OF JACKSON HOLE

TIM SANDLIN

BlueChip Publishers

Printed in the United States of America.

Print ISBN 978-0-930251-02-4
Ebook ISBN 978-0-930251-03-1

BlueChip Publishers
Jackson Hole, Wyoming
BlueChipPublishers.com

Contact the publisher at info@BlueChipPublishers.com

Find Tim Sandlin's fan page at facebook.com/timsandlinpage

First edition

For Carol

Special thanks for Mike Sellett, Adam Meyer, Kevin Olson, and James Joseph

CONTENTS

INTRODUCTION

At some vague point in the 1980s — pioneer days — I was copy editor for the Jackson Hole News. Late one Tuesday night as we finished putting the paper to bed we discovered a hole on the Letters to the Editor page. Holes in the Letters to the Editor can't be filled with an honor roll list or the rules of snowmobile maintainence. It has to be a Letter to the Editor.

So I changed myself into Kathy McLish and wrote a Letter to the Editor about the white stuff on the mountains being Styrofoam so the climbers won't get hurt when they fall. To my amazement, readers thought the letter was real, and I like to think if social media back then wasn't two old cusses hollering at each other though the gap between pickup trucks, I would have gone viral.

Thus, the Pyms column was born. What I did was I created a raft of people who lived, loved, laughed, and fought for the next seven years or so. I could argue both sides of any issue, so long as both characters were wrong.

The column brought about a certain number of near lawsuits and three death threats (death threats are not something you say certain number about), but for the most part, life was good.

Then I made the mistake of writing a column about writing a column. First law of the columnist: When you write a column about writing a column it's time to quit.

The *Rite of Passage* ended with the publication of The Pyms: Unauthorized Tales of Jackson Hole. *You can order a copy from your local independent bookstore or the Internet Guys or tim@timsandlin.com.*

I stopped writing 52 columns a year and switched to two — summer and winter — for the fine folks at Jackson Hole Magazine. *I did it a couple years, then someone else funny took a turn, then in the mid to late 90s I came back and I've been with the magazine twice a year ever since.*

What we have here is a sociological history of the last thirty years in Jackson Hole. Not so much accurate factually (I write fiction) as truthful in attitude. Most of my predictions didn't come true, thank goodness, but this is what those who came before now thought mattered.

When I first arrived in the Tetons, the Park Service was in a tizzy as to how to deal with 60,000 tourists a summer. Now, it's four million and the tizzy hasn't changed. Traffic still sucks, housing is awful, billionaires have chased out the millionaires, locals ski, fly fish, hike, drink, and argue relentlessly against anything new. No one wants progress in their own backyard.

What I discovered, rereading these things, is a pattern where I would write a column about a controversy and twenty years later write another column about the same controversy — controversy never changes around here — and I would accidentally steal from myself. Who can recall what they wrote 20 years ago?

The careful reader of this book will notice a pathological obsession with the theory that Old Faithful is fake. And frequent references to the five-hour Yellowstone vacation. And the shabby treatment of non-skiers by skiers. Children of the main characters' names change between 1991 and 2017.

That's how history works. The past is fluid. Memory is muck.

My advice is to read this book slowly. Leave it in your guest house or bathroom. One chapter should be enough to help you sleep at night.

Take it as educational or recreation reading. It represents decades of wonder.

Tony DeLoney (as she sold me a rock from her back yard) once told me Jackson Hole had gone steadily to hell since the late 1920s, but no matter how bad things get in the Hole, it's still better than anywhere else.

Tim Sandlin
September 2021

1988

The University of Heidelberg recently commissioned Dr. Hugo Papagosi to come to the United States in order to make a systematic study of the lifestyles and mores of the natives here. It was decided that, in order to fairly choose a study area, Dr. Papagosi's graduate students would stretch a Rand McNally map of the U.S. across the back wall of a biergarten and the doctor would fire a dart from a distance of forty paces. Wherever the dart landed would be the chosen study area for this team of crack sociologists.

Dr. Papagosi's dart pierced the map at a point in Wyoming midway between Jackson and West Moose. Thusly, last winter saw the arrival in Jackson of twelve highly-trained social observers from Germany. You couldn't open your mouth without someone sticking a tape recorder in your face. It was disconcerting to locals, and, frankly, we breathed a collective sigh of relief when Dr. Papagosi and his study team packed up their portable computers and data bases and returned to the land of Volkswagens and braunsweiger.

Nothing was heard from the sociologists for eight months and we almost forgot them. Then, in last week's mail, I received a copy of Dr. Papagosi's findings. Some of the words came out muddled in the translation from the original German, but I believe the gist of his conclusions are intact.

According to Dr. Papagosi, there are twenty-four layers of society in the valley, ranging from the true descendants of Nick Wilson, founder of Wilson, Driggs, and the first owner of the Stagecoach Bar, to horses and tourists.

I quote Dr. Papagosi: All social systems seem to be based on an "us" and "them" theorem. "Us" may easily be defined as me and anyone who loves the Tetons as fervently as I do, but the term "them" has evolved into a very personal concept based on this idea. Everyone who came to Jackson Hole after I did is not a true local. For those born in the valley, outsiders are everyone who came after their first ancestor arrived. The only truly-accepted "local" in the valley is a 102-year-old Arapahoe woman named Blue Shovel, now living in a Road King mobile home in the B&B trailer court.

Of the 10,000 plus residents coming after Miss Shovel, my colleagues and I have broken the society into 24 separate segments.

1. Gorpers — Named for an almost indigestible food they consume, this group skis twelve months a year. Their only mode of transportation is the mountain bike on which they think nothing of riding to San Francisco on a weekend to catch a Grateful Dead concert.

2a. Granola snappers — Also named for their diet, but sometimes called Yurpies because of their tendency to live in Yurts and tipis. Yurt people feel vastly superior to tipi people and vice versa. This group also has an unnatural interest in mountain sports, but, as opposed to Gorpers, these folks can see the sunset over the white water, so to speak. All clothing is bought used or if it is new, they claim it came from well-meaning relatives in Ohio. Whereas a Granola Snapper is proud of never having seen The Shootout, a Gorper doesn't know what The Shootout is. Granola Snappers put an inordinate emphasis on signs of the Zodiac.

2b. Hummers — Subgroup of granola snappers who climbed the Sleeping Indian for the dawn of the Harmonic Convergence and spent the day buzzing Om at each other.

3. Trust fund babies — Generally found on stools at the local bar. They enjoy darts and silent art auctions.

4a. Hollywood syndromes — Named because they've seen too many movies, these are stockbrokers, lawyers, CPAs from Back East who gave it all up to come live the simple life where the air is pure and the Cerveza organic. They have a tendency to subscribe to the *New York Times* and stand on rocks at sunset, yelling, "What ho, the glories of leaving the rat race."

4b. False Hollywood syndromes — Left the rat race before joining it. They drink scotch and say things like, "I could be making $80,000 a year if I'd stayed in Chapel Hill."

5. Nellie Belles guys — Winter and summer, they drive mud-covered 1956 Willys Jeeps.

6. Prairie dog Dundees — Australian cowboys. May be spotted by their jeans tucked inside their boots and better than average posture.

7. Ninety-day wonders — Summertime seasonals. When first confronted, they always say, "Where you from?"

8. 120-day wonders — Winter seasonals. Marked by facial tans dark as a Vasque hiking boot broken by a blank newsprint-colored band across eyes and ears caused by goggles. Interestingly enough, neither 90-day-wonders nor 120-day-wonders believe in the existence of each other.

9. Grizzly Adams syndromes — Often from New Jersey. They long to dwell in the mountains and commune with animals and water and rocks. May be subdivided into a) real mountain men who prefer to eat their elk poached and b) wimpy mountain men, vegetarians who think if they are gentle enough baby deer will lick their faces and grizzly bears will perform circus tricks.

10. High tech wienies — These people spend thousands of dollars on top-of-the-line equipment before ever attempting a new sport. One woman we studied bought a twelve-hundred-dollar F-2 windsurfer, two wet suits, a dry suit, three sails and a custom-designed roof rack for her Volvo before discovering she didn't like water up her nose. This same woman purchased her three-year-old son a Stump Jumper 15-gear mountain bike with training wheels.

11. Old timers — Easily spotted by their thick sweaters with Conestoga wagons and bull elk on the back. General talk centers around the winter of '42 and the New Pass Road.

12. Fly heads — For this group, life is centered around mayfly hatches on the Firehole River. Can spend days discussing double-tapered 2X floating lines or fish that they didn't catch. They do not actually eat fish because a dead trout is one that can't be caught again. Each Fly Head has total disdain for anyone who doesn't fish by the same technique that he does.

13. Drunks — Anyone who stays indoors on a nice day.

14. Children of the Triad Religious — Cult centered around Emma Matilda Lake. This cult believes the Tetons are hollow with a kingdom inside ruled by Edgar Cayce, Marilyn Monroe, and Elvis. They feel that if they hold their mouths in a certain manner and recite the words of Jimi Hendrix's "Foxy Lady" over and over that they will be given admittance to the Triad Kingdom through a cave under the Jenny Lake Lodge kitchen.

15. Cowboys — May be broken into four subgroups: a) Cosmic or Drug Store — will buy jeans only with snuff-can-print prepressed into the right back pocket. Often ride snowmobiles and chase women from Salt Lake City, b) Rodeo — generally lack teeth and limp badly, c) Ranch — these cowboys actually work with cows. They often wear red-neck caps and sneakers out of a fear of being mistaken for truck drivers, d) Hunting Guides — know a lot about rifles and knots, they dislike anyone from Pennsylvania or for gun control.

16. Tree huggers — Derogatory name given to environmentalists who think the plants and animals of Jackson Hole are more important than the economic welfare of the humans.

17. Stump sucker — Term used by tree huggers to define anyone who uses the term tree hugger.

18. Realtors — One of our researchers attended a Realtor coffee klatsch and became so bored she had to be hospitalized. Even now, months later, our researcher must go to a physical therapist once a week to stimulate glazed-over sensory organs.

19. Sick jocks — Athletes who whip themselves into such finely-tuned machines that they suffer almost continual colds, flu, and forms of the grippe. Our study group found healthy people are ill up to four times as much as sedentary slobs.

20. First Church of the Second Hand — Religion based on recycling consumer goods. Members become sexually excited at the sight of a garage sale and will often buy back items they donate to thrift stores.

21. Wildlife biologists — Probably the most prevalent group in the valley. These people have irresistible compulsions to get up at four in the morning and go out to count things.

22. Bert's birders — Named for their leader, this cult has forsaken all semblance of comfort and hope for a normal life in the impossible pursuit of something called a "life list."

23. Migrating Bagos — Often older, these people follow the ancient circle from Phoenix to Jackson Hole every year in their large buslike homes. They have an unnatural fixation on the outdoor barbeque and if approached suddenly, are likely to fend off strangers by whipping out photographs of their grand-children.

24. Crazy — What the other twenty three groups consider anyone who doesn't live in Jackson Hole.

SUMMER 1991

Dear Delores,
        You don't know me but I'm from Oklahoma and I used to be married to your sister's husband, Tobias. I'm remarried to Johnny Roy Ledbetter now and we lease the Bojangle's Chicken franchise in Velma-Alma. Chicken's been good to us, Delores.

I ran into Crystal and Tobias at Surplus City last week. She said she's been drinking three quarts of cranberry juice ever day for a month and that infection she got from the toilet seat at Howard Johnson's still won't go away. I told her my mama swears by Massengill and prayer.

Anyway, J.R. and I are touring America this July on our Kawasakis and Tobias suggested we stop by and visit with you and your little family. We will arrive the evening of July 10. Would you be a sweetheart and reserve us a room in a motel for that night and maybe three more. We need a swimming pool, a good ice machine in the room, a view of the Titons and a coffee shop with real ice tea, not the instant kind.

Johnny enjoys the Magic Fingers but if you can't get that you can't. We're not picky. The only thing is we refuse to pay more than 22 dollars a night.

Tobias says if we can't find a motel that meets our standards we could probably stay with you a few days. J.R. and me won't be a lick of trouble. We'll be quiet as mice. I'll amuse myself with the soaps and J.R. just fools around with his precious motor bikes.

If you could get time we'd love to travel Yellowstone with some real pioneers who know all the little cafes where tourists don't go.

I should warn you I am allergic to milk products.

Yours with sugar, Jimmie Sue Dockett

Dear Jimmie Sue,

I was so glad to hear from you. Tobias has told us about you for years. We lit a special candle when your husband got out of jail three months earlier than ya'll expected.

We wouldn't think of letting you stay in a motel. Peter has been looking for someone to help him regrout the basement and the kids love it when guests stay over in their room. We'll move the baby in with us and you can sleep on Cora Ann's floor while Johnny Ray takes the couch.

It's funny that your letter came this week because Peter was after me to write you and ask for a loan for our new business. We're opening a shoe museum — Footwear Through the Ages — and we know you'll want to be in on the ground floor.

There are many wonderful restaurants and lounges in the Jackson area, and, if we count our pennies, the four of us can have a fine night out on the town for under 300 dollars. Peter and I don't want you all to spend too much money on us.

I truly admire your courage in riding motorcycles through Yellowstone after that problem with the bears last summer. It gives me the honest willies when I think about the mother grizzly pulling that poor woman out of the sidecar, ripping her open, and eating her small intestine. The woman didn't even pass out — just lay there watching that bear suck her guts up like a teenager slurping spaghetti.

She's fine now, happy to have lost the weight.

There is one downer to staying with us. You might want to bring extra A-200 because of the lice thing. Peter thought they were tiny spiders until the doctor said we had to shave Cora Ann's head.

Come on out though. We'll get through it all and laugh afterwards. We just love having people we don't know stay at our house in the summer.

Sincerely (with sugar), Delores

WINTER 1991

Fifty or sixty times a winter I have the same conversation with someone in funny-colored pants.

Funny-Colored Pants: "So, how was the mountain today?"

Me: "I heard Toilet Bowl was bulletproof, but Hoop's Gap was soft, the lower faces corn and the top of Thunder bumps was totally rad for shredders. Dilly Dally Alley was all glaze and Corbet's was champagne-powder-and-snorkel snow. Wally World was nothing but smoke."

FCP: "Sounds wonderful. Where did you ski?"

Me: "Me? I don't ski."

FCP (After giving me a look usually reserved for dead rats found floating in the commode): "Why do you live here then?"

Why do you live here then? What a rude question. If I'm in L.A. and meet someone who doesn't drive a car, or Miami and meet a person who doesn't deal crack, do I sneer "Why do you live here then?" Of course not. I might look at them funny but I'm much too sensitive to question their very right to exist.

Jackson Hole is paradise and anyone who doesn't live here is nuts, as far as I can tell. In summer the valley is a vast playground, in fall it's the most beautiful locale on the planet, with weather that is the standard by which all other weathers are judged. Winter is beautiful, soft, and peaceful — a time of quiet contemplation, of reading and thinking. In most of the country thinking has been replaced by malls.

Then in spring everything melts to mud and the locals go on vacation.

The schools are good, hospital fine; we have a symphony, art museums running out our ears, and seven — count 'em, seven — movie screens. Skiers drinking margarita-flavored schnapps in their outdoor hot tubs don't believe it, but Jackson Hole has churches and Cub Scouts and video stores, even a public library. A person can live a rich, full life here in Wonderland and have absolutely no contact with snow other than looking out the window now and then to murmur, "Gee, isn't that pretty."

The one, the only, drawback to this good life is the athletic stigma of non-skierdom. We're treated like lepers.

I was minding my own business in the post office one afternoon last winter when Heather Heidi Walsowski-Smith crunched up in her Salomon Space Invader boots and raccoon tan. "Where are you skiing this weekend?" she asked.

I looked down at my sweepstakes notices and pizza parlor coupons and mumbled, "I don't ski."

She was dumbfounded. *"WHAT?"*

"I don't ski."

Heather Heidi shouted, loud enough for the whole post office to hear, "Hey, everybody, this guy doesn't ski."

Grownups giggled. Children stared. One woman crossed me off her Christmas list. I felt like a rhesus monkey in a research lab. The crowd turned and watched as I walked down the line of post office boxes and out the glass doors.

Roger Ramsey caught up with me as I reached my car. "You're either courageous or stupid," he said.

"I feel so alone. I've been ostracized by the Town Without Pity."

"Tim, you are not alone."

I searched his face for a sign of sarcasm. "You mean . . . you don't ski either?"

"Swear on a stack of trail guides you won't tell anyone."

"I swear."

"I can't stand skiers or skiing."

I was so happy. "That means there are two of us."

Roger looked at me a few moments, sizing me up for trustworthiness. "Come on," he said. "I'll show you something amazing,"

Roger led me down a dead-end street, over a fence to a narrow alley, into a courtyard where we passed through an unpainted door down dark steps into a basement. He stopped at another door and rapped out the drum break from "Satisfaction" by the Rolling Stones.

"You're not going to believe this," Roger said.

The door was swung open by a woman wearing blue jeans and a T-shirt. Inside the large, comfortable room people were reading and playing chess and discussing movies. Couples held hands as they gazed into the crackling fire in the fireplace.

At first the place seemed like regular Jackson society, but then I noticed something really weird. Their clothes — no Day-Glo, no Lycra or Gore-Tex, no thousand dollar Bogner jumpsuits with prissy bibs. These people reeked of normalcy — shirts with buttons, Wrangler jeans, hats you wouldn't wear to rob a bank.

"My God," I said. "I'm in the Twilight Zone."

Roger led me toward the fire. "You are in the sanctuary of NIDS — No, I Don't Ski. Everyone of these people is just like you and me."

A woman came up and asked if I wanted a cup of coffee. No cappuccino laced with Jaegermeister or psychotic mushrooms or anything. Just plain non-skier coffee. As we talked she asked about my work and told me her daughter had a part in the school play. We discussed the situation in Iraq. Not once did she mention wax.

It had been so long since I had a conversation that didn't revolve around slope conditions that I was struck dumb. I kept expecting her to say "totally radical." This was a dream come true for me. Most women in Jackson Hole would rather French kiss an earwig than date a non-skier.

Roger told them the story about Heather Heidi asking me where I was skiing this weekend and everyone had a good laugh, but I didn't mind because they weren't laughing at me like the mean people in the post office. This was more like a support group sharing a joke.

"The first rule of NIDS," said the woman I'd been talking to, "is never, ever, tell the truth to a skier."

"What should I have said to Heather Heidi?"

Each non-skier had his or her own line for getting out of tight spots.

"I haven't been able to sit on a chair lift since my vasectomy."

"The network won't let me. My Lloyd's of London policy expressly forbids skiing and bullfighting."

"I'm allergic to snow. One touch and I get cold."

"Since I discovered bungee jumping, skiing is too boring."

"I'm hunting grizzlies with a spear this weekend."

"I'm flying to Paris with Susan Sarandon."

"My church doesn't allow standing on boards with members of the opposite sex."

"I blew my knees on the gelande. Want to hear the details of my operations?"

"Elvis told me not to ski."

One man pointed to his crutches propped in the corner. "I use those all winter whenever I'm in public. Nobody hassles me."

"How do you handle skiers?" I asked Roger Ramsey.

"The groovy people don't listen anyway. Whatever they say, I just grin like I'm stoned and answer 'Bitchin', man.' Everyone takes for granted I'm a snowboarder."

1992

Professor Anton Slaassen, world-renowned for his studies of eating disorders among the Samoans, recently spent three years in northwest Wyoming, observing the living patterns of members of the Polypropylene Generation. After recording hundreds of native oral histories, Dr. Slaassen discovered a clear pattern concerning the rites of passage in a tourist-based economy. It is his thesis that this cultural pattern can be applied to other outposts of the Lycra mentality, such as Taos, Moab, Steamboat Springs and Sun Valley.

While adolescents follow one of two angles of entry — either summer, in the form of a seasonal job for a national park concessionaire; or winter, the traditional semester off school to ski — by the end of the first year, both tracks come together in a specific life course.

If you are a new arrival to paradise, according to Dr. Slaassen, here is what you have to look forward to:

2nd summer in the valley — You live on national-forest land and work in the service industry to support your sports habits. You tell your parents it is temporary, a phase you are going through before returning to the "real" world. You fall in

love with a co-worker because he/she has similar sporting interests and a waterproof tent.

2nd winter — You live in a condo with five others of your
peer group. You work two jobs and develop a habit of binge
drinking beers and sweet liqueurs no one back home has heard
of. You break up with the seasonal sweetheart and go on to
sleep with six partners in six months, at least one of whose
name you will never learn.

3rd year — You initiate a steady, year-round romantic relationship. You buy sheets and stop sleeping on a mattress pad
covered with a sleeping bag. You find a job that does not
require working weekend nights.

4th year — After threats from the parents, you return to
college for a semester. You do well in school but live for the day
you'll see the Tetons again. You tell your father that Jackson
Hole is out of your system; your mother knows better.

5th year — You return to Jackson Hole. Now when you use
the term "home," you mean Wyoming. For the first time, you
own a car that is worth more than your bicycle.

6TH year — You blow out a knee in the mountains.
Blowing a knee in Wyoming is similar to the circumcision ritual
among the Samoans; it is the line at which a youth becomes an
adult. Those who never blow a knee appear, in Dr. Slaassen's
observations, never to grow up.

7th year — In a sudden spurt of responsibility, you buy a
block heater for your car and get married. The outdoor ceremony is performed by a large, bearded man known for being in
touch with the earth.

8th year — You move to Teton Valley, Idaho, after your
new spouse convinces you that it is too expensive to live in
Jackson Hole unless you are single; and, if you're not, what's the
point?

9th year — You move back to Jackson, still owning no
insurance or stock portfolio. At your high-school reunion the
kids you graduated with look five years older than you. They no

longer have metallic objects piercing their noses, lips or breasts.

10th year — For the first time since moving to Jackson Hole you have more money invested in clothing than in footwear and sunglasses. After being cut off financially by your parents, you prove your maturity by steaming all of the drug and alcohol decals off your snowboard.

12th year — You buy studded snow tires, a sure sign of middle age.

15th year — You give up pot and Jägermeister for Ibuprofen and Mylanta.

20th year — You are 40 now, the traditional year when Jackson Holites are expected to have children. So, you do.

23rd year — You win the affordable-housing lottery and buy a starter home for only $450,000.

25th year — You break it to your parents that you will probably stay in Wyoming for longer than originally intended.

35th year — You and your spouse move out of the starter home and into a million-dollar, two-bedroom cabin with Teton views.

36th year — You divorce. Your spouse gets the million-dollar cabin and you move into a condo downstairs from six kids who are in the Second Winter stage of the life cycle.

40th year — You marry someone you slept with the first six months you were in the valley.

41ST year — Your parents move to Jackson Hole so you can take care of them.

42nd year — You child tells you nature is repulsive and he/she is moving to Seattle to develop computer systems by day and play electric keyboard in a noise band at night. You are expected to finance the move.

45th year — You start listening to the same scuzzy music you listened to that first year in the valley. You go on a buying spree on the Internet and recreate your entire album collection from freshman dorm. (Females will often skip this stage.)

46th year — You sell all your mountain-climbing equipment, your kayaks and everything to do with nonmotorized flight. You migrate south for four months of the winter.

50th year — You blow out a hip on the slopes. This is considered the ritual end of mid-life and the beginning of old age.

1993

Two weeks ago there was a story in the local newspaper about a woman who works for the Main Street Association and she said that the Square should move away from "rubber tomahawk" stores. Then last week they had a story about "the rubber tomahawk king" of downtown Jackson.

I said to Peter, "What's all this rubber tomahawk jive? There hasn't been a rubber tomahawk for sale on the Square in eight years. You think that Main Street woman has actually been in a downtown store?"

"It's just a saying, Delores. It means a store selling things to tourists that they don't particularly need - like shot glasses with a picture of Old Faithful, or lacquered slabs of driftwood painted with cute sayings like 'World's Greatest Fisherman,' or 'Anywhere I sit my guests, they always like the kitchen best.'"

"Why not call this guy the Lacquered Slabs of Driftwood King, then?"

"It's a saying, like white-collar worker. White-collar workers haven't worn white collars since 1962."

"Mormon missionaries and waiters at the Village Inn Pancake House wear white collars."

"They're blue-collar workers. Take the 'granola snapper.'"

"You take the granola snapper."

"I never met a granola snapper who even eats granola. And God, Himself, doesn't know what the snapper part of that term means. America is full of terms that say one thing and mean something else."

"Like 'amateur athletics' or 'military intelligence', or something like that."

Nevertheless, I went to the Square in search of the elusive rubber tomahawk. Not a store up there — including the six owned by the rubber-tomahawk king of Jackson Hole — sells rubber tomahawks. What I did find was a busload of Asians setting up tripods and zillions of dollars of camera equipment, all aimed at the elk horn arches.

This struck me as odd. In a county with Jenny Lake, Mount Moran, and Harrison Ford, why throw all that energy into photos of the Rocky Mountain version of a McDonald's sign. One guy seemed to be in charge — he was the only one smoking a cigar — so I walked over and introduced myself.

His name was Wallace Tofu. He works for Cowboy Joe Tours of Tokyo.

"So what's with the arch obsession?" I asked.

"In Japan, the elk horns are ground into wafers and sold for $200 an ounce. We use them as an aphrodisiac."

"That's $3,200 a pound. There's 20,000 pounds of antlers on the Square. That figures to... "

Mr. Tofu whipped out a Casio calculator and punched some buttons. "That's $6,400,000 worth of aphrodisiac on display in the Town Square. How would you feel if you were touring Japan and in a small village you came upon six million dollars worth of cocaine piled up on the ground?"

"I could relate to this better if it was six million dollars worth of Patsy Cline records."

"You're not getting the point, Mrs. Pym."

"Peter would like six million in Debra Winger posters. Have

you ever been in bed with someone and realized they're pretending you're someone else? It's like fantasy adultery."

"Mrs. Pym, imagine you're touring Japan and find $6,400,000 worth of *anything* sitting out in the open."

"The Cheyennes were really into animal parts. If elk horns are an aphrodisiac, they'd have known."

"We put it in our tea."

"Can you imagine a first date in Tokyo. The boy tries to slip the girl a little horn. She slaps him in the face and screams, 'I don't do horn.'"

"You think we're silly for spending money on elk horns, but all these people on my tour are here as a reward for a record-breaking year at their factory."

"What does their factory make?"

"Rubber tomahawks."

WINTER 1999

I took my pen and pad and went down to the nicest rock on the shore of Jenny Lake to sit in the sun and observe that most elusive Jackson Hole species—the tourist. Tourists are wonderful. Imagine the entire population of an area whose sole purpose for being there is to have fun.

And, for the most part, they pull it off, which is truly amazing when you consider the bizarre, alien environment they're forced into—fathers hurled together with children they haven't seen in fifty weeks, American children without television, mothers without microwaves or telephones. Against all odds and contrary to the common myth, most tourists enjoy themselves.

However, like Christmas, compulsory fun brings out the weird in a few, and these few were my quarry. I searched for the Dysfunctional Tourist and I found him. Here, without further sociological mumbo, are actual transcripts of actual tourists doing whatever it is people actually do on vacation.

Middle-aged guy in Haggar slacks, Polo shirt and Rolex, hollering at four kids: "We didn't drive 1,500 miles for you to feed Oreos to a damn bird. Get over here and appreciate this beauty."

The kids play jump-from-rock-to-rock-in-the-lake games. The littlest one falls in, and his sister yells in a voice like cutting cardboard with a butter knife, "Smooth move, Exlax."

A bus load from the Golden Rule Club of the Jayhawk Methodist Church in Osawatomie, Kansas, unloads by the ranger station. A woman whose hair appears as a blue helmet says, "If I have to ride one more minute next to Genevieve Parsons, I'll scream. Twelve hundred miles she's been going on about her gallstones. I've got gallstones. We all have gallstones. What makes her so special?"

Lady in a sweatshirt showing a run-over bear saying, *All I wanted was a cookie:* "I wonder what they do with the mountains in the winter."

Husband has on white Florsheim shoes with little tassels: "Thirty-six bucks for a T-shirt. I can't believe you spent thirty-six bucks for a T-shirt. You don't even wear T-shirts back in West Covina."

"It's machine washable."

Three college-age-looking girls come by. A blond in Guess hiking shorts and an Eddie Bauer sweater whines, "I can meet a man in a bar and smell him and just tell that he's a Sigma Chi."

Girl whose teeth glitter with braces: "I'd give every bear in Wyoming for a mall right now."

Two other women come down from the bus. They sport tight hair buns, dark hose and nurse shoes. The word "matron" comes to mind. I imagine these women drinking Ironport and eating radishes. The short one approaches.

"What is this place?"

"Jenny Lake," I say.

She turns to the tall one. "Jenny Lake." The tall one looks in a travel book.

"It's not listed."

"It's got to be listed."

"We're not supposed to be here if it's not listed."

"Look under 'natural wonder.' "

"Here it is." The tall one makes a check mark; they whirl and leave. The odd thing is that neither one so much as glances at the lake and the mountains beyond.

The guy's wife is wearing a Frank Shorter jogging suit and about five pounds of turquoise jewelry. She smokes a long, brown cigarette: "I'm going to burn those comic books if Monty doesn't look out the window soon."

A woman in a Texas A&M sweatshirt and earrings with an A in the left ear and an M in the right: "I told you the elk turn into moose when they grow up."

Man with a cap made from Coors cans: "I saw an elk hunting show on ESPN, and they didn't say anything about that."

"The ranger said elk turn into moose in their fifth year."

"Seems strange to me."

"Rangers don't lie, Chester."

A man parks a Ford van, and eight blond kids and a beagle pile out and run squealing onto the boat dock. He stands next to his van, sipping a Diet Pepsi: "We saw everything there was to see in Yellowstone in five hours. Tetons shouldn't take more than one."

His wife has on Bermuda shorts, a down parka and flip-flops: "I can see the Tetons, but where's Jackson's Hole?"

A Mini-Winnie pulls up, Louisiana plates. Out steps a woman with her hair in pink curlers, and a man with the toes cut out of his sneakers and a tattoo of an alligator on his fore-arm. She says, "They say the white stuff is snow but it's really Styrofoam so the mountain climbers won't get hurt when they fall."

Man scratches an appendix scar: "If I see one more lake, I'm gonna throw up." A girl with three hundred dollars invested in her boots and seventy-five cents in the rest of her outfit gets off the Cascade Canyon commuter boat. She has pigtails and a yellow bandana on her head. The guy with her is dressed exactly the same, including the pigtails and bandana.

The girl: "One of the new age thinkers out in Kelly died yesterday."

The guy: "Huh?"

The girl: "He had a dry mouth and drank four gallons of Celestial Seasons Sleepytime tea."

The guy: "Huh?"

The girl: "He was found drowned in his teepee."

The guy: "Huh?"

WINTER 2000

N ostra-Sandlin of the Weather Channel Forecasts the Third
Millennium

2000, January 1 - At midnight of the new millennium, the
Y2K Bug shuts down Old Faithful geyser.

2000, March - In order to protect its billion-dollar investment in the Old Faithful complex, Yellowstone Park Co. hires
technicians from the Bellagio Casino in Las Vegas to replace
Old Faithful with a new, even more-faithful fountain. A government and private cover-up keeps this a secret from the public
for over 150 years.

September - A purple cloud from the Idaho National
Engineering and Environmental Laboratory drifts over Grand
Teton and Yellowstone national parks.

May - Twelve two- headed buffalo are born in Lamar Valley.
A federal commission investigates and finds no connection
between this and the event of the previous September.

2005, summer - Property values in Teton Pines and the
west bank of the Snake River plummet as wealthy former Californians flee Jackson Hole. The Chamber of Commerce investi-

gates and finds no connection between the housing market and the two-headed buffalo. The housing shortage remains desperate in the rest of Jackson Hole.

2020 - Kelly, Wyoming, is declared a celebrity-free zone, one of two in the United States.

2032 - The last remaining wolf in Yellowstone is killed by a retiree taking part in an antique Winnebago rally.

2050 - The dean of the College of Jimi Hendrix Studies at the University of Wyoming quits his job in a huff when he discovers that the men's football coach is being paid more money than he is. The state legislature appoints a committee to investigate the matter.

2051 - Jackson attempts to solve its housing problem by building a huge subterranean condominium complex beneath the site of Albertsons' fifth store in Jackson.

2052 - Unfortunately, none of Jackson's workers will live underground, so the condo complex is converted into real estate offices.

2056 - Dick Clark retires from the "American Bandstand."

2065 - Jimmy Strathmore of the Greater Wilson Metroplex talks on a cell phone in front of a stranger from New Jersey — little knowing she is a postal worker with PMS — thus becoming the first person killed on the Grand Teton since the elevator system was built.

2069 - Wyoming becomes the first state in the union to take away the male's right to vote. Governor Sylvia Simpson says, "They didn't use it, anyway."

2088 - The United States follows Wyoming's lead and disenfranchises the male population. In a related incident, male-to-female sex-change operations are now a felony (no one wants the other kind).

2098 - Wolves are reintroduced to Yellowstone National Park. Local politicians predict that it will be the end of the family farm.

2112 - A disagreement at the end of a college basketball game escalates into the Utah–Wyoming War. Ethnic cleansing in the Evanston area climaxes in the burning of 300 beehive hair-dos.

2116 - Justine Peters of Moran wins a purple ribbon at the Teton County Fair for her 82-pound zucchini squash. She is later disqualified for using plutonium in her plant food. Fair judges catch her when they notice the squash glowing at night and old "Blind Lemon" Fuller guitar licks emanating from the core of the gourd.

2150 - The National Star exposes the Old Faithful cover-up; riots break out across the nation. Several bears are hung in public places. Cynicism runs rampant throughout the world.

2198 - Grand Teton National Park initiates an environmental impact statement (EIS) on what effect closing the park dump will have on the raven population.

2206 - The Rocky Mountain tourism business goes tits up after USA Today reports fewer mosquitoes and shorter lines in the Backcountry 2.1 version of the virtual-reality family vacation.

2215 - After sex is outlawed in California, border guards and dogs are stationed at the Wyoming state border crossings. When refugees are asked why they didn't just stop in Utah to have their sex, they reply, "What?"

2217 - The so-called "Hundred Year War" between Utah and Wyoming ends after the Battle of Dutch John, with the signing of the Cowboy Joe Treaty, in which Utah admits that the point guard's foot was on the line.

2220 - A Jenny Lake cabin maid works the entire summer and is still a virgin.

2222 - After a tragic accident involving the Golden Rule Club of Wichita, Kansas, and a secret barbecue sauce, wolves are once again removed from Yellowstone.

2241 - The Grand Teton EIS on the effect of closing the park dump on the raven population is cut short by the death of the last raven.

2301 - Three French tourists having lunch at Colter Bay Village leave a dollar tip. One returns later to ask for change.

2321 - Tobacco smugglers are captured on Union Pass and subsequently hung on the last Douglas fir standing along the Gros Ventre River.

2330 - Fish tacos are voted the national food and riots break out in Paradise Valley, Montana. The government commission investigating finds no connection between the two.

2341 - All rodents are removed from the Greater Yellowstone Ecosystem. They are considered unnatural, exotic species.

2375 - Ending 150 years without carnivores in Yellowstone, an experimental program allows a small group of lawyers to enter the national park.

2376 - Angry buffalo stampede, killing all the lawyers in Yellowstone. A memorial is erected honoring Jeb, the leader of the buffalo.

2410 - Rumor has it a wild child has been seen in the Teton Wilderness, but the Forest Service denies the possibility. Head forester Billy Joe Bobby Jack (BJBJ) Webster is quoted as saying, "We ain't had wild children in Wyoming since one little bugger gave a tourist woman fleas back in '89. She sued our pants off and we had to poison the lot."

2450, winter - Temperatures bottom out at 92 below zero, freezing every hot pot and geyser in Wyoming. This is recorded in Yellowstone history as "the year hell froze over."

2450, summer - Bicycle paths are finally installed in Grand Teton National Park.

fall - Wyoming elects a Democrat to the U.S. Senate.

2580 - A Delta Airlines flight arrives in Jackson Hole on time, with every passenger's luggage aboard. The Catholic Church investigates the miracle in preparation of naming the pilot, one Murray Frappuccino, a saint, but Murray is disqualified for telling jokes over the plane's P.A. system.

2600 - During the century celebration at the Cowboy Bar, the Town Square bubble is accidentally burst, allowing snow to fall on downtown Jackson for the first time in three-hundred years.

2611 - Once again, as prophesied in the Book of Cycles, two Frenchmen eating at Colter Bay Village leave a tip.

2801 - Students at the Kelly School discover an ancient manuscript complete with an alleged photo of a tree. Their teacher tells them it is a hoax.

2830 - Continuing the tradition of building a new high school every 20 years, the valley opens Jackson Hole High School number forty-four.

2888 - The Shoot-Out Gang celebrates its 100,000th performance on the Town Square by vaporizing the Cache Creek Posse.

2999 - A tourist from Lower Georgia throws a millennium commemorative coin into Morning Glory Pool, plugging the underground steam system and resulting in the explosion of the Yellowstone Caldera and the total destruction of everything within 500 miles of the Mammoth snack bar, with the exceptions of coyotes, mosquitoes and the miniature golf course at Snow King Resort.

SUMMER 2001

When I was but a youth, the ranger conducting the Jenny Lake nature talks told this joke: Scientists wanted to compare the relative ferocity of Alaska mosquitoes and Wyoming mosquitoes. They found that a man trapped in a room with ten Alaska mosquitoes could not escape without being bitten. Unfortunately, when they tried the experiment in Wyoming, they were unable to find a room with only ten mosquitoes.

Today's Jackson Hole High School students wouldn't get that joke. In the late 1970s, the county government began an annual spraying of Malathion, which wiped out the mosquito population. The purpose was to foster tourism, boost property values and help make life in the Wild West hassle-free. The program was a raving success. Today's Teton teenager — who spends little time outdoors, anyway — may well have never known the delicious itch of a mosquito bite. Today's kids do not know the intense satisfaction that comes from leading a persistent mosquito on until she feels secure in her conquest, then squashing her into oblivion

But all of this carefully contrived insulation from nature may go down the tubes this summer. The Environmental

Protection Agency has found Malathion in Teton County's water. The EPA called up Teton County Weed and Pest and told them that if it happened again they would be fined $5,500 per incident.

TCW&P didn't like this. After all, the mosquito is not a pest, legally, in Wyoming, and it isn't a weed anywhere. TCW&P was spraying the poison only as a favor to the county government. So TCW&P went to the Teton County commissioners and said, "We can't do it anymore." The commissioners said, "If you won't do it, we'll find somebody who will." TCW&P told the commissioners that mosquitoes could be controlled legally and safely with larvacide, as opposed to Malathion adultacide, but larvacide costs more. Costs are a big thing with the commissioners. Now they are out looking for new sprayers, but no one seems willing to absorb the $5,500 per incident fine. The commissioners can't understand why all of these westerners have turned into wimps in the face of the federal government. They're hoping the California power shortage will give the new president justification for dumping all of the silly environmental safeguards and it'll be okay to spray poison in the county again, no matter what those EPA whiners say.

Jackson Hole now finds itself split into three political groups: 1) the Malathion-is-harmless/get-the-feds-off-our-back bunch, 2) the larvacide-is-safer-and-worth-the-money group and 3) a small but vocal mosquitoes-won't-kill-you faction.

In April, the interested parties met in the basement of the Wort Hotel to discuss the issue, like neighbors. Clyde Walsowski-Smith led the pro-poison party. He trotted out several old-timers to tell what a living hell Jackson Hole had been before spraying. For more than two weeks during most summers, they said, you couldn't even drink a beer outside in the evenings. No billionaires bought land in the Snake River flood plain and built houses on top of the swamp, on account of the flood plain was uninhabitable. Clyde said, "If we don't spray poison on all our standing water, the billionaires will go some-place where they do."

Clyde's wife Heather Heidi said, "That's the point.'

Clyde said that at the moment there are 79 properties for sale for over a million dollars each in the valley and 22 for over five million, and that practically all of those properties are in prime mosquito habitat. "What will we do with the mansions if the billionaires leave?" Clyde asked. "Turn them into dormitories?"

Clyde meant this as sarcasm but he got a standing ovation anyway. Patty McMulers, speaking in favor of larvacide, said that even though her program costs three times as much as the Malathion program, at least it's legal in eyes of the EP A, and if we didn't kill the mosquitoes there'd be no tourists.

Heather Heidi said, "That's the point." An anonymous hankie-head pointed out that Yellowstone National Park doesn't spray for mosquitoes and they have plenty of tourists. "That's right," Patty said, "but they have swallows, bats, plenty of trout, and aerosol cans of OFF on the grocery store shelves, none of which we've had since we started killing mosquitoes."

Crystal Amber Free-Spirit — a known tree-hugger with braided armpit hair and a business that produces natural deodorant out of pine nuts — asked why Jackson has the highest concentration of six-toed babies outside Kosovo. Clyde shouted back, "What's wrong with six-toed babies? You Califor-nians come here and think you can change everything. Why don't you go back where you came from?"

Crystal Amber started crying and said she was born in a yurt in Kelly and that she'd never been to California. She said she'd heard that if we didn't stop killing mosquitoes, the Forest Service was threatening to stick them on the endan-gered species list. "That would serve you blood-suckers right," she cried, totally mixing her metaphors. She was booed soundly by the pro-poison faction. The evening ended on a sour note when the Right to Life bunch got in a fight with the Fund for Animals coalition and the NRA shot out the lights.

While the county commissioners fight over what to do about the problem, the Chamber of Commerce has asked me to publish a flyer with helpful tips on what you can do to protect yourself should you ever encounter a mosquito in the wild. I'm quoting myself now: Do not panic. The mosquito can smell fear. Gather information before taking action. Remember, only female mosquitoes bite, so, first, ascertain the gender of your mosquito. The females have sharper tongues and tend to bigger hips as they age. If the butt glows, it's a lightning bug and not a mosquito. Lightning bugs make interesting bracelets when squished around your wrist.

As the mosquito bites, observe its rear end. If the rear end is vertical to your skin, this is the breed that carries malaria. They should be avoided. If one is already in you, allow it to continue siphoning blood until it sucks its own poison back into its body, at which point you may smash it with the palm of your hand.

As a child, I recall letting several mosquitoes gorge at once, then smearing my arm into a bloody streak, thereby grossing out any grown women in the vicinity. This was before Sony PlayStation 2, when children were expected to entertain themselves.

After the mosquito has flown off to use your blood as a host in which to lay her eggs, thus creating a million more mosquitoes, the bitten spot on your skin will itch. Your mother will tell you not to scratch the itchy spot. She will say that scratching will only make it worse. Like everything else your mother tells you about safety in nature, this is a blatant lie. Why would the human body come with itches if they're not a signal that you should scratch? Ignore your mother. Scratch the hell out of that mosquito bite. Scratching yourself raw is the only fun part of the experience.

One last safety note: While mosquito repellent and bear

repellent look similar, they are applied differently. This lesson was learned the hard way last summer by the Nordstrom family of Tyler, Texas. While camping at Grant Village, Wynona Nordstrom told her children they could not go out to play until they lined up for a proper dousing of bear protection. Those wishing to contribute to the Nordstrom Fund should sent their donations to the Zion Children's Hospital, Box 1000, Salt Lake City, Utah 84132.

WINTER 2001

Jackson Hole has the youngest old-timers of any valley in the West. Anyone over 22 who has been here at least three years considers himself qualified to tell a newcomer, "It's nice enough now, but you should have been here before people like you ruined it all." After the topic of billionaires displacing millionaires and ruining paradise, old-timers' second favorite subject is how much worse the weather used to be. To hear them talk, each winter was colder and the snow deeper all the way back to 1911. Before that, exaggerations set in and memories can't be trusted.

Roger Ramsey was telling me the coldest winter he ever lived through was 1978-79, when it hit 64 below zero on New Year's Eve and spit bounced. Tires squared, key holes jammed solid, anti-freeze froze, the electricity went out, and several hundred people piled together in a heap in the lobby of the Wort Hotel.

"I've been in sixty below temperature and sixty below wind chill," Roger said, "and trust me, sixty below temperature is colder. Wind chill doesn't mean squat unless you're outside naked."

What I remember about 1979 was the 155 degree difference

between New Year's and the Fourth of July. People who live in states where weather is not the central element of life can't relate to a 155 degree temperature swing.

Because of a childish prank up Crystal Creek involving a paintball gun, a sow grizzly, and the Vice President, Roger Ramsey was recently given a choice between jail and 100 hours of community service. He chose the latter.

His service entailed going up to Pioneer Homestead, where the real old-timers live, and taping oral histories for the Living West in Memory Program, a National Public Radio show on which myths and legends of mountains are set straight. I joined him on his first outing there, where we found Caleb Johnstone, T.R. Whitlock, and Betsy Rae McAlester nodding out at a table in the Homestead courtyard, each facing two one-dollar bills, a Delaware Punch, and one of those bruise-colored peanut-and-sugar patties that are shaped like a hockey puck and have the shelf life of a belt buckle. Roger says old guys eat them for the preservatives.

Roger set up his Radio Shack voice-activated tape recorder, and, as usual, conversation sprang up on How Cold Was It.

Caleb Johnstone ran his finger bones over a head so bald you can see the separate skull plates, and reminisced about November of 1951:

"They was a flock of sandhill cranes bedded down the night in Christian Pond there, and the temperature dropped from forty above to forty below in two hours flat. Froze ever one of those bird legs solid as angle iron in concrete. Next morning, they was pitifulest bunch of birds I ever saw. But then, right while I watched, this big old crane that seemed to be the boss bird commenced to flapping his wings and all the other cranes flapped their wings and pretty soon the ice broke free from the banks and that flock rose into the sky, carrying the top eighteen inches of Christian Pond with them. Looked like a municipal ice rink floating in the air above Jackson as they crossed town and headed south.

"I heard that ice didn't melt free 'til the flock was passing over the Odessa, Texas, stockyards, where it crashed down in one huge slab. The Texans never knew where it come from, but they had such a mess of pounded meat under ice that they went out and invented chicken fried steak."

T.R. Whitlock stared at Caleb with one eye so wide open it looked like a glowing Ping-Pong ball. "Fall of 1951 wasn't near as cold as late March 1942," he said. "That was the spring Molly Van Dyke brought a little bottle of sorghum molasses to the Moran School to pour over biscuits during recess. To stop the molasses from firming, she kept it under her armpit all morning, but come recess Budder T. Olaf got to teasing her and he threw the molasses bottle and broke it on the bicycle rack that used to be a hitching post."

"Does this story got a point?" Caleb asked.

T.R. blinked his Ping-Pong-ball eye. "After we went back indoors for elocution exercises a grizzly bear that's just woke up from winter-sleep came out of the woods and took to licking the molasses off that bicycle rack. First we knew of it, that bear busted through the double front door with the rack and my little sister's ruby red Flexible Flyer bicycle stuck to its face.

"It ran up and down the room, knocking over desks and chairs and the living terrarium with the hibernating snakes and the live iguana. Some of the girls let loose in their pants and what with the doors open that froze the floor slick and the bear fell and slid into the blackboard. Miss Hankfield grasped her Wonder Bread ruler."

"I remember that ruler," Caleb said. "It had 'Wonder Bread Builds Strong Bodies Twelve Ways' on one side and on the other they'd written one way per inch."

"Who's telling the story?" T.R. said.

"Don't tell it if you can't do it right," Caleb said.

"Miss Hankfield reached across the bicycle rack and cracked

that bear on the nose. It ran clear out the back end of the coat closet and into Pacific Creek. Carried a good number of jackets with it, but lucky for us my sister's bicycle fell off. We got away with a flat tire on the front."

I couldn't help myself. "So, what happened to the bear?" I asked.

"Nobody knows," T.R. said. "There was stories going around of a bear with a wide set of iron teeth terrorizing the DuNoir that spring, and in late June a cabin maid at Lake Hotel found the bicycle rack out by the dude corrals. It had a pink tongue stuck to it."

Roger Ramsey turned a whiter shade of pale. "That's not the end of the story though. A year later Molly Van Dyke married Budder T. Olaf and for forty-three years she made him pay for that molasses, every night and every day, till the good Lord finally said enough and called Budder T. home."

Betsy Rae spit something green on Roger's Nike. "Cold is one way to judge a winter," she said, "but I prefer snow as a gauge of harsh." Betsy Rae claims to be 112 and there are those who believe her. She is considerably older than Caleb and T.R. That much is true. More than 80 years of working outdoors in Wyoming has turned her skin the color and texture of a snapping turtle's.

"Nineteen and twenty-two," she began. "The tallest building in Jackson was the four-story, two-hole outhouse behind the clubhouse there on Center Street."

She spit again but this time Roger was ready for her. She continued, "The men of our town were too lazy good-for-nothing to shovel snow, so they'd just let it drift over the first floor, then open the door to the second floor and so on until mid-April, when the snow started back down and so did the men."

She poked Roger with a scaly fingernail. "That Christmas, your greatgrandaddy Jug Ramsey — he wasn't no more account than you are — rode his mule Frankie in from the upper Gros

Ventre. Jug left Frankie out back in a howling snowstorm and went inside where he got caught up in an all-night domino tournament. Whiskey was involved. And a crib girl from Elk.

"The next morning snow had piled up neck high to a tall blacksmith, as they measured it back then, and Jug couldn't find his mule. He looked for two days until he became convinced Frankie would turn 'Up in the spring,' so Jug headed home up the Gros Ventre before the next storm.

"What Jug and no one else knew was Frankie had somehow taken shelter in the first floor of the outhouse. Snow piled up so deep that winter four floors wasn't enough. They ended up cutting two holes in the roof and stretching a canvas tarp for privacy. When spring finally did come, the snow melted down floor by floor until folks noticed an odor worse than usual.

"I'll never forget the sight if I live to be 115. Frankie was packed in there so tight they had to peel off all four walls. People came in from miles around to see that donkey, and the *Police Gazette* even sent out a photographer. The men never used that outhouse again. The next year they not only built an indoor water closet but they let responsible women join the club."

Like a fool, I asked, "Did the *Gazette* run the story?"

Betsy Rae nodded. "You betcha. Right on the front page they had a picture of Frankie looking for all the world like an eight-foot Fudgesicle with hooves instead of a stick, and the headline there read: 'Jackson Men Can't Tell Ass from Hole in Ground.' "

Silently, Caleb and T.R. pushed their dollar bills across the table to Betsy Rae. Roger turned off the tape recorder. "I'd' rather go to jail," he said.

WINTER 2002

On the last warm day of September, Roger Ramsey and I walked over to the Brewpub to check out the fall halter-top hatch.

"Is it my imagination," Roger asked, "or are we seeing more cleavage this year?"

"Girls in the middle of the country are dressing like they're in L.A. now," I said. "It's a Britney spillover."

Roger eyed a girl in a red tube thing around her top and jeans hanging from her pelvis. His viewing was strictly in the interest of fashion awareness, I assumed, and in no way reflected sexist objectification of women. He asked, "How do you think she holds her britches up?"

"Duct tape," I said. "The sticky-on- both-sides kind."

"I thought maybe it was glue."

We found Roger's cousin, Simon, at the end of the counter, staring glumly into a twelve ounce glass of Snake River Lager. "You look like your ex-wife got custody of your dog," Roger said. Simon drained his glass and said, "I think I caused an international incident. You boys may want to clear out before CNN shows up."

Simon is a fishing guide, and that week had been guiding

Vice President and faux local Dick Cheney down the South Fork of the Snake River. It's a time-honored tradition in America that presidents golf and vice presidents fish. Dick Cheney is a fisherman with ambitions to play golf. The way I know he has such ambitions is because he owns a house out at the Teton Pines golf course. If he was happy to stay Vice President, he would have bought on the river.

It doesn't seem plausible, to me, for an international incident to be triggered on the South Fork — I mean, we're talking Idaho here — and I said as much to Simon.

He said, "That's what I thought, too," and then proceeded to tell us the story of the war nearly caused by a number-twelve Double Humpy.

"We were floating along a pretty stretch of the river between cottonwoods and willows, me and Dick at the center of these concentric circles made up of twelve more guides and oarsmen, a veritable cadre of Secret Service agents, a personal secretary, a press secretary, assorted advisors, spokesmen, and go-fers, a communications team manning satellite hookups, computers with wireless Internet access, and a global positioning system in case we got lost on the South Fork, a press pool of eastern elitists freezing to death, chefs, pilots, and convoy drivers, and a man with a black suitcase holding the code for initiating a nuclear attack. Two double-rotored Huey helicopters whock-whocked overhead, and, above them, three F-16s kept the skies safe for fly fishing.

"It costs the government a little over a hundred thousand dollars an hour for Dick to feel like he's by himself in the wilderness," Simon added.

"I did the math on that cup of Kool-Aid that Bill Clinton bought from those kids on Spring Gulch Road when he was out here," Roger said. "It came to a half-million dollars of taxpayer money for a twelve-cent paper cup full of grape sugar water."

Simon took a deep chug of beer and waited. He hates to be interrupted when he's telling stories. Finally, he went on.

"Enos Thurston was in the boat behind us with the cultural attaché from Georgia."

"Georgia doesn't have culture," Roger said.

"It's the Georgia over in Russia. The Bush Administration wants to make it the fifty-first state. Their plan is to turn all those trouble spots over there into states and wire them for cable TV."

"But we already have a Georgia," I said.

"They plan to change the Russian Georgia's name to Cheneyland. North and South Yemen are going to be Bush Junior and Bush Senior."

"That's reasonable."

Simon continued. "I told Dick to drop his Double Humpy over behind a low-hanging log, where I predicted he'd catch a big cutthroat. It wasn't such a wild prediction as you'd think on account of I'd been feeding two twenty-inch cutthroats in that hole Double Humpy-shaped dog food for a month."

"Where do you find Double Humpy-shaped dog food?" Roger asked.

"You carve it from Kibbles 'n Bits. Are you going to listen or ask questions?"

"I'll listen."

Simon looked at me and I said, "Me too."

"Well, Dick's a proud man and he allowed he'd rather fish the willows. He plunked his fly into the willows where it instantly got hung up. I could have told him it would but Dick won't listen to me since the FBI found out I'm a Democrat."

Roger started to say something but Simon gave him a shut-up look. "I said we ought to break the leader but Dick said the Double Humpy was a present from the king of Finland or someplace and it had sentimental value, so I had Enos row into the willows and lean out of his boat and pull the willow aslant so Dick could snap her out of there. Only Dick snapped her into the cultural attaché from Georgia's left nostril."

"Ouch," I said.

"Don't hurt that much," Simon said. "I've hooked myself plenty of times. Half the girls in here have pierced noses."

Looking around, I confirmed that many of the halter-topped women had indeed stuck sharp objects through their nostrils, apparently by choice.

"But this attaché acted like we'd slid a splinter under his thumbnail. He screamed and grabbed the strike indicator and fell on the floor of the boat."

"What'd Dick do?" Roger asked.

"He commented on how pretty the willows were with the leaves changing. But his press secretary got worried that they wouldn't change the name of Georgia to Cheneyland, and the secretary commenced to chewing me out, and the press pool boat carrying reporters from *O* and *Vanity Fair* floated up and the photographers saw blood and started taking pictures and the press secretary yelled at the Secret Service boys to stop them, so this one Secret Serviceman took an oar and knocked a camera into the river, so the photographer knocked the Secret Serviceman into the river and that yellow coiled wire in his ear shorted out with a pop I could hear clear across the channel. From what I understand, the Secret Serviceman still can't hear from that ear.

"Dick opened a can of Albertsons Cherry Cola and sat down to wait for things to mellow out, only sitting down jiggled his rod tip and that made the attaché yell like a bull being turned into a steer.

"About then Dick's doctor floated up. He had enough doctoring gear on that boat to do a heart transplant, but nothing for pulling a number-twelve Double Humpy with a barbed hook out of a Russian's nose. Enos had to loan him a needle-nose pliers."

"Wait a minute," I said. "I read that the Vice President fishes barbless."

Simon looked embarrassed. "That's disinformation they give the press. Truth is, we'll work our way down the political correctness scale to whatever it takes to land a fish. I even carry a top-secret box of worms, in case of an emergency."

Roger was amazed. "The Vice President fishes with worms?"

"It hasn't come to that, yet. Worms are like nuclear bombs. We don't plan to use them, but they have to be there."

I said, "Does the attaché still have a Double Humpy in his nose?"

"They got it out right after the red phone rang."

"You didn't tell me about the red phone."

"It only rings in times of national crisis. The press secretary jumped to get it. He said, 'Yes, sir' four times, held the phone out to Dick, and said, 'It's the President.'

"Dick said, 'What's George Junior want this time?' and took the phone at the same moment as the doctor squeezed off the barb and the attaché screamed and the humpy flipped across the river carrying a piece of Georgian nose, where it landed behind the overhanging log and was taken by one of my twenty-inch trout."

"This is getting hard to believe," Roger said.

"Tell that to the Secret Service," Simon said. "They're blaming me."

"I'll bet Dick went with the trout instead of the President," I said.

"Of course. The cutthroat jumped clear of the log and Dick struck with both hands on his rod, which was great except he dropped the phone in the river."

"Where's the fish now?" I asked, keeping my priorities in order.

"They did a photo-op for the guy from *Vanity Fair* and we released it. Dick always fishes catch-and-release. We're real careful about that."

"Did you find out what the President wanted?" Roger asked.

"They never tell me squat. Last time he called I found out it was about a barbecue sauce recipe."

"I guess Cheneyland won't be joining the union," I said.

"Hell, the Russian army is mobilizing."

"Did the Vice President say anything to you about the incident?"

"He says if there's a war, he's shipping me to the Baltic Sea."

"What for?"

"I'll be the designated hostage."

SUMMER 2003

L ast June Delores and I hiked up to Inspiration Point in Cascade Canyon. A pair of osprey were fishing the base of the creek, where it flows into Jenny Lake, and bringing their catch to a nest perched like a cliff condo where three baby osprey waited with open beaks. It was a nifty sight and we watched the birds for over an hour while various members of the tourist set marched up the trail from Hidden Falls.

After a bit, two ladies of the senior persuasion came panting up the trails in red Keds and t-shirts that said Biloxi Baptist Golden Rule Adventure Club. The one had hair the exact color and consistency of an SOS pad. The other appeared to be wearing a bicycle helmet made from recycled Coca Cola cans, but she wasn't. It was all her.

After the two ladies collapsed onto rocks the blue-haired one twisted her fanny pack to the front and took out a guidebook of the Tetons. She said, "What is this?"

The redhead looked around until she saw the sign that read "Inspiration Point. Do not go beyond this point." She said, "Inspiration Point."

The blue hair clicked her Bic and marked a check beside Inspiration Point in the guidebook, then they both turned and headed down the hill. Neither woman so much as glanced at the lake, much less the valley below.

Delores said, "Don't you hate checklist tourists?"

I said, "Hate is kind of a strong word -"

"They're worse than checklist birdwatchers." Delores has a major peeve with checklist birdwatchers. She considers competitive bird watching events as immoral, even nastier than parking in handicapped slots when you aren't handicapped.

"It's the opposite of watching," she told me during one virulent tirade. "It's bird identifying, then not watching. It's bird ignoring."

For me, the sign of a successful marriage is taking your mate's obsessions seriously even though you think they are silly. Personally, I don't care if people want to count species. It keeps them out of politics.

As the checklist ladies headed down, a pot-bellied guy in a black leather coat, black pants, and what Californians think is a cowboy hat came puffing up the trail with a hundred pounds of photographic paraphernalia. He actually had a tripod for the camera and a bipod for the fence post of a lens. I watched as he screwed this to that and adjusted a host of micro-variables. At no time did he stop to enjoy the view.

"I was with Clyde Walsowski-Smith in Lupine Meadows last week," I told Delores, "and he kept trying to force me to look at a photo he'd taken of an elk."

"Hard to think of Clyde as caring about elk," Delores said.

"That's the point. There were four real elk standing in the meadow right in front of us and Clyde didn't care. He was more interested in exploring the simplicity of digital photography."

"Clyde's one of those people thinks an experience didn't happen unless he records it," Delores said.

The pot-bellied man glanced up, momentarily. I like to think he was seeing the conversation flying over his head, but he was probably checking the light.

Two six or seven-somethings came jumping from rock to

rock up the trail followed by a worried mother in her mid-twenties, a father in his mid-forties, and a sullen teenage boy -- obviously a trophy wife/stepmother situation. I made this guess based on the teenager's shirt that read "You're not my real mom." Somebody, the father, I suppose, or it could have been the first wife bent on revenge, must have forced the kid into this vacation on the theory that it would be educational. I have never seen anyone so determined to avoid taking in information. He stared at his footwear and when the blond stepmother said, "Look at the prairie dogs, Brad," Brad refused to look.

The younger kids proceeded to feed caramel corn to what they claimed were prairie dogs but were actually incredibly overweight golden-mantled ground squirrels.

The father said, "Look at the lake dammit, I didn't drive fifteen hundred miles for you kids to feed rats."

The little ones ignored him; the teenage sulker ignored him; the trophy wife ignored him. She was terrified the kids would hurl themselves off the cliff, so she wasn't about to look at anything but them. The mental picture of riding days in a car with this gang was enough to see why the traditional family vacation has gone the way of the whooping crane.

One of the kids bumped into the photographer's camera, which caused him to emit a mild curse.

The father said, "Watch your language."

The photographer said, "Watch your brats."

Delores said, "Let's throw the camera and kids off the edge and see which one rolls into the lake."

A couple came from the canyon side of the trail. The guy was so intent on studying his satellite location device that he stumbled on a rock and almost fell into the camera, which would have caused more friction.

The woman said, "Look where you're going."

He said, "I want to see where we are."

"The sign says we're at Inspiration Point."

He didn't look up from his PDA. "The sign might be wrong."

Three mountain climbers trudged past, each carrying ropes, pitons, crampons, and a pack as big as a Volkswagen Passat. The front one looked straight down at the trail and the other two looked at the calf muscles of whoever was in front of them. They went by silently, like ships.

About that time an intense young woman with three hundred dollars invested in her shoe and sunglasses and fifty cents in the rest of her outfit plunked down on the rocks and lit a cigarette. She tore open her Land's End daypack and pulled out a blank, lined-paper notebook with a cotton flower pattern on the cover and commenced to journaling. This girl journaled hard and long. The faster she wrote, the deeper she puffed on the cigarette, until a veritable cloud surrounded her intense head. I imagined she was recording her feelings, impressions, reactions, and anger for posterity. You could almost see the black void of her formless soul washing across her designer diary. What the woman wasn't recording was anything outside her own skull. She never once looked up except to glare at me for looking at her.

"I'll bet she's a radical feminist," I said.

Delores said, "Amazing. Did you see that?"

"What?"

"The osprey stole a trout from an eagle."

"I missed it."

"You missed it. How could you miss it?"

"I was people watching."

"We came on this hike to immerse ourselves in nature. You want to watch people, we'll go to Albertsons."

"Good idea."

WINTER 2003

As we all know, there are five new golf courses under development in the Jackson Hole area, on top of the two luxury and three regular-guy courses already here. Which got me to wondering — why? Our beautiful valley is snow-covered at least seven months a year, followed by the thirty-day drizzle in May or June. That leaves four months of decent golfing weather — not much compared to Hawaii or North Carolina — and these resorts aren't cheap to develop. It takes a lot of cash to turn grass green in Wyoming.

So, where's the profit? We live in the outdoor recreation capital of the world and I can't imagine how chasing a ball across a pasture would rate in the top-ten fun activities. You can chase balls just about anyplace where you can see the ground, which means anywhere but ski areas and parking lots. But with outdoor sports based on mountains, snow, or crystal-clear water, why are ninety-five percent of the investment dollars going down the golf hole?

Clyde Walsowski-Smith knows everything there is to know about turning paradise into a commodity, so he was the man to see. I found Clyde loading his Lexus RX 330 SUV with skis, golf clubs, road bikes, mountain bikes, two canoes, a DVD player, a veritable Sundance catalogue worth of resort wear, and his laptop Dell computer. He also had a machine called a Blueberry that as near as I can tell is for talking to people who don't talk to people.

When he saw me standing there, Clyde said, "Vail."

I said, "What?"

"Vail is installing heated pipes under the streets. They'll have a winter without driving on snow or ice."

He showed me the article he'd clipped from the *Jackson Hole News&Guide*. A Vail councilwoman named Diana Donovan was quoted: "Now, we won't have snowplows scratching up the streets, leaving big piles of dirty snow, or going *beep-beep-beep* all night and waking up the tourists."

"Imagine," Clyde said, "a ski area with permanently dry roads. There will be no disadvantages left. They will have made Vail as comfortable to live in as Parsons, Kansas."

"And just as interesting," I said.

Clyde paused in the midst of checking his cell phone voice mail. I think he suspected that I was resorting to irony. I flashed him my sincere look, which isn't that sincere, but it generally passes if the person I'm flashing it at is vacuous.

Clyde said, "Remember when we were growing up and September to June was 'Cocktail Hour in Jackson Hole' because there was nothing to do but drink? Then the ski area came in and our daylight hours were filled with healthful recreation, only there aren't that many daylight hours here in winter, which left two-thirds of each day divided between drinking and sleeping around."

"Old-timers call that the 'golden age of Jackson Hole'," I said. "Sternum-deep powder all day followed by fruit-flavored brandy and wide-shouldered women with raccoon-face tans all night."

"Boring," Clyde said. "But then we were given Mexican restaurants and franchise delivered pizza, cable TV, video stores, seven movie screens instead of one that kept the same movie from solstice to equinox, and suddenly people are living in town who don't give a hoot for outdoors. The only drawback is half a year of skating rinks for streets, and Vail has solved that. If it works, I'm going to come back here and convince the commissioners to tear up every road in Teton County."

"I haven't seen any roads lately that aren't already torn up," I said.

"There's an alley in East Jackson, hasn't had a flag man on it in three years."

"Okay," I said. "But with our unique opportunities for fishing, biking, hiking, kayaking, paragliding, mountain climbing, four kinds of skiing, hunting, snowmobiling, and, my favorite, sitting on a rock beside a babbling creek, why are all the development dollars going into a sport you can do anywhere and do it year-round other places?"

"You mean golf?"

"I mean golf."

"Not enough rolling profit in the other sports. Once you drop a bundle on equipment, mountain and river sports are practically free. The more you hike and fish, the cheaper it is. With downhill skiing and golf you pay for your privileges every time out."

"But golf doesn't make sense in a valley with seven or eight months of snow cover."

Clyde pointed to a bumper sticker on the back of his Lexus RX 330: *Doing my part for global warming.*

"Golf is our hedge," he said.

"Against what?"

"Let's burn some fossil fuels," which is what Clyde says now when he wants to go for a drive.

Clyde started the SUV and said, "Teton Village." The vehicle's GPS unit, which occupied the space where the radio should have been, retorted, "Drive 300 yards and turn left." The voice was that of a well-dressed woman, kind of like a receptionist about to put you on hold.

"I hate these things," I said.

Clyde seemed surprised. "But I never get lost anymore."

"It's been years since I got lost between Jackson and Teton Village."

The woman said, "Signal and move to the left lane."

"It's a wife-in-a-box," I said. "You should bring her instead."

"I have to feed my wife."

As we drove out to the site of the proposed golf estates, Clyde explained why the government isn't doing anything to stop global warming.

He said, "Deep down, most of us actually like the idea of a warmer planet. You notice they don't call it global heating. It's warming. Who can knock warmth?"

"What about the forest fires and drought?"

"Environmentalists cause the forest fires, and droughts sound bad but I'm not a farmer. I don't even know any farmers. Fire and drought don't change the average citizen's day, right now. Warmth does."

"There's six countries in the South Pacific that claim they'll be under water in thirty years."

"Worrying about countries in the South Pacific is Democratic handwringing. Given a choice between shoveling snow off the roof and drowning Pago Pago, real Americans will drown Pago Pago."

"And in fifty years when New York and L.A. are under twenty feet of salt water?"

"You say that like it's a negative."

"Those millions of people aren't going to go away. They'll move up here."

"And play golf," Clyde said, winking.

The well-dressed woman said, "You passed your turn. Go back immediately. Turn around now. Turn back at once.

Clyde reached down and slapped a switch on the GPS, shutting off the voice. He said, "That's another thing you can't do with a wife."

SUMMER 2004

After parking off the Gros Ventre Road, shrugging into his sixty-pound Kelty pack, and strapping on snowshoes, Roger Ramsey commenced slogging for two days up and over the divide to reach Toppings Lake for the melt out. The snowshoes proved fairly useless in the infamous Gros Ventre gumbo, mud the consistency of dark molasses mixed with shampoo. But, for Roger, the thought of being the first of the season to catch and release a grayling on a barbless dry fly was worth the suffering.

Breathing like a London stalker, Roger finally came across the ridge and dropped down to upper Toppings Lake, where he found a helicopter parked in the meadow. A family from Santa Barbara was enjoying a picnic — father, mother, two boys, and a nanny — all dressed in Sundance catalog-wear and dining on a baby shell pasta salad with calamata olives and roasted fennel. The grown-ups were drinking Nouveau Beaujolais from crystal wine glasses, the nanny was over in the willows smoking a joint, and the boys were yanking grayling from the lake as fast as they could poke a worm on a hook.

Roger charged up to the family and told them he was a Forest Service backcountry ranger. He demanded to see their permit, and when the father produced one, Roger tore it to bits. He then Swiss Army knifed all the rubber hoses on the helicopter. He smashed whatever could be smashed with rocks. He stuck the kids' fishing poles in chiseler holes, broke them off at the reels, and threw the pieces in the lake. He set the worms free, then said, "You're fired," to the nanny.

Little did Roger know, the phrase, "You're fired," had recently been copyrighted by Donald Trump. (I am not making this up.) Roger was arrested by a real backcountry ranger and hauled into Teton County Court, where he was sentenced to community service — which he claimed he'd already fulfilled by attacking the helicopter — and five sessions in Maurey O'Hara's group therapy class, "Rage Control for Nature Buffs."

Roger was nervous about going to the class by himself. He has a history with Maurey O'Hara. They'd once been married for six days, until Maurey let it slip that she liked Abba better than Merle Haggard. The divorce was semi-ugly.

Roger talked me into going with him. "I don't need rage control," I argued.

"I do," Roger said, "whenever I see Maurey."

We found Maurey and three other court-ordered class participants in the back room at the Hard Drive Cafe. In order to protect the privacy of three people who are known for their angry ways, and who might pound me if I used their real names, I will call them Larry, Curly, and Mo. Mo is a woman.

Maurey had a flannel board holding a photo of the Dalai Lama at the top and a sign that read: "We play outside in order to relax." First, she had us close our eyes and say along with her, "Nature is beautiful. Nature should be fun," three times. I caught Roger peeking at her as we chanted. I don't think he'd yet reached stage four in the grief process regarding their marriage and divorce.

"What does recreation mean?" Maurey asked. I started to speak up, but she gave me a look that said she would supply her own answer. "It means to recreate. To enjoy life. To be refreshed by the natural world. And yet, for you folks, and many others, recreation leads to conflict. Why is that? Why don't each of you tell me why, when you should have been in your most blissful state, you wound up under arrest?"

Larry, whose real name isn't Larry, went first. "I was hiking along Cache Creek with my black Labs, Flopsy, Mopsy, and Cottontail, when a mountain biker came flying down the road, completely out of control. He swerved to miss Cottontail and did a face plant in the dirt while his bike tumbled into the creek."

"Were your dogs on leashes?" Maurey asked.

Larry ignored her. "The jerk blamed Cottontail. I couldn't believe it. He cursed my dogs and when I told him to mellow out, he cursed me. Then he kicked Flopsy."

"How did you deal with your inner emotions?" Maurey asked.

"I did what anyone else would have done. I emptied a canister of Udap Bear Deterrent in his face."

Curly, meanwhile, had soloed the Grand on a beautiful day in June only to find a North Carolina internist on top, talking on a cell phone. "Not just taking," Curly said. "He was yelling, 'Hey, Norma! Guess where I am? I'm standing right on top of the Grand Teton!' The yahoo mispronounced Teton. When he said 'TEAT-on,' my mind snapped."

"I would have thrown his phone off the Grand," Roger said.

Curly nodded. "I did that, along with his Palm Pilot, Global Positioning System, MP3 Player, hands-free headset, and his boots."

I had to ask. "Why the boots?"

"Whenever I mug a person, first thing I do is take their shoes. That way they can't chase me afterwards."

Mo is a photographer. She tracked Bear No. 162 across the Lamar Valley for three days, until one dawn when she found the grizzly feeding on a coyote carcass down by the river. "It was a cosmic moment," Mo said. "Fog rolling off the river, steam at the bear's nostrils. The light was religious. For once, I had the proper telephoto lens. It was the shot of a lifetime."

"How did you feel at that moment?" Maurey asked.

"Perfect inner peace. I was at one with my universe."

"And?"

"And Colby Potemkin walked out of the timber and into the clearing, directly into my frame, waving his pocket instamatic like he was signaling a plane to taxi up to the terminal. I prayed the bear would kill him, but my prayers were not answered. Instead, the bear took off over the ridge. Colby came huffing back to where I had my equipment set up, and he said, 'Heavy, man.' "

"How did you feel then?" Maurey asked.

"I changed my views on gun control."

"Did you resort to violence?"

"Of course not. I waited. I stewed. Three weeks later I ran into Colby at a Fund for Animals potluck. I heard him telling some Wilson bench people the story of how he and animals communicate by ESP. He said, 'Bears are my brothers.' "

"How did that make you feel?"

"I creamed him in the face with a plate of eggplant lasagna."

"Why is it," Maurey said, "that we go into nature to find peace, joy, and bliss, yet, so often, we discover the opposite?

"Because idiots get in the way," Roger said,

Maurey slapped her hand to the flannel board. "Exactly. If you put two people on a ridge top with a Disney sunset and air so pure it makes your lungs ache, each of those people is going to wish the other wasn't there. That won't happen in a New York City subway."

"That's because paradise should be perfect," I said. "A New York subway is hell to start with, so no fool in an I'm With Stupid t-shirt can possibly ruin it. But they can sure as heck do a number on paradise."

Maurey told us to gather in a circle and give each other hugs.

"Last time we did that there was a fistfight," Mo said.

"That's before I started a separate session for hunting guides. Now, I want everyone to hug."

Afterward, Maurey, Roger, and I went to the Brewpub for a dark lager. The way Maurey and Roger were google-eyeing, I suspected they might work out the Abba dilemma. But I still didn't understand. "Why does natural beauty bring out the violent streak in people?" I asked.

"I break my clients into two groups," Maurey said. "Inter-sports and intra-sports. Snowmobilers and cross-country skiers are natural enemies, like Republicans and environmentalists. Each group denies the other's right to exist. Horse riders and hikers. Para-motorists and everyone else."

"What's a para-motorist?"

"Paraglider with a lawn mower engine on the back. We've had a spate of topless sunbathers shooting at them down on the river."

"Those make some sense, but I don't follow intra-sport violence."

"Violence within sports is much more rabid. Your expert anything — mountain climber, wind surfer, fly fisherman — has contempt for the inept. Many sportsmen think that no one who's not as good as themselves has a right to even practice a sport. So, when the expert has to wait, or change plans, because a beginner is on his turf, the expert reacts with scorn. He taunts. He shouts, 'If you can't do it, get off the mountain.' Or out of the river, or whatever. You'll never see a neophyte attack an expert. It's always the other way around."

"So, what's the answer?" I asked.

"Outlaw tourism," Roger said.

Maurey shook her head. "Then you'd feel free to assault any local who came here after you did."

"Maybe we should all move to Alaska," I suggested. "Nobody gets in anybody's way there. Everyone is happy."

"The crime rate in Alaska is fourteen times that in China," Maurey said.

"Okay, let's ship the valley to Hong Kong."

"It could get even more violent," Maurey said. "If the developers get their way, we'll soon be infested with golfers."

WINTER 2004

Heather Heidi Walsowski-Smith came into Pearl Street Bagels to pick up a half-caff skinny vanilla no-foam double latte for the road. She told me her husband, Clyde, has volunteered to play Santa Claus for storytime at the Wee Britches Day School next week.

"Isn't Clyde a bit scary to play Santa?" I asked.

"It's his scotch-imploded nose. The tiny red blood vessels make him look jolly when he puts on a full, white beard."

"I've heard Clyde described many ways, but never jolly."

"He is now. Ever since Columbine started pre-K, Clyde is a whole new man. He cares deeply about organic milk and violence in cartoons."

I don't know what's happening out in the rest of America because I haven't left Teton County since the Clinton years, but here in the mountains there's been a veritable epidemic of 50-year-old fathers of toddlers. You go to a Mighty Mite soccer game, and the crowd looks like bone density testing day at the assisted care center. You think to yourself, isn't it nice, all these grandpas babysitting the little ones, until you realize the silver-headed geezers on cell phones are the dads. Never in county history have there been so many old men with so many young children.

Let's say roughly half of this over-the-hill-but-still-watching-"Sesame Street" bunch are like Clyde. Clyde took a semester off college in 1970 to come west and ski, and he never quite went back. His 20s and 30s were spent on sports — climbing, kayaking, bicycling through South America — which in his 40s bled into fly fishing and golf. His mid-life crisis hit at 45, but what was he going to do? Ski again? Instead, Clyde found Heather Heidi waitressing at the Brew Pub and convinced her parenthood would give direction to an otherwise pointless life.

The other half of the diaper duffers are like Bill Bonnell. At 20, Bill moved out of his tipi and went to work in his father's ad agency in L.A. He worked like a compulsive obsessive on Ritalin for 30 years, not slowing down until he was a filthy rich man with a hiatal hernia, a clogged heart, and a prostate like a balloon in the Macy's parade. He also had a 25-year-old son he didn't know. So Bill dropped $4 million on a ranchette and a Hummer and settled down to do it right this time. He's the kids' coach.

I wanted to see this new, gentle version of Clyde, so I stopped by storytime at Wee Britches. I have a daughter there myself. We adopted her from China by traveling on our AARP discount card. She's the cute one.

Nine 3 and 4 year-olds dressed in Lands End toddler wear sat in a circle on carpet scraps while their teacher, Miss Periwinkle, introduced Clyde as Santa.

Clyde came out doing the *Ho Ho Ho* bit, and his daughter Columbine burst into tears.

Miss Periwinkle rocked Columbine in her lap until the girl got over the shock, when Clyde went into the act.

"Good morning, boys and girls!"

The kids weren't buying it. They sucked on sippy cups and clutched blankies and stared at this fat man in red like he was an earwig in the bathtub.

"Tell us how you've been this year, Santa," said Miss Periwinkle. "What's it like at the North Pole?"

"I don't live at the North Pole anymore," Santa said. "Mrs. Claus and I bought a condo on Flat Creek so we could be near the elves."

Miss Periwinkle wasn't sure what to say on that one. Personally, I've never approved of the Man Who Gives Away Free Stuff mythology. I told my granddaughter Krystal he was a creative writer's personification of Christmas cheer created by the toy industry to indoctrinate the infant market and instill guilt while maximizing debt load in adults. She told me her favorite color is purple.

"We've outsourced Christmas," Santa said. "The toys are being assembled in Indonesia, and the letters are handled by child labor in Lithuania. Most kids send e-mails now anyway."

"Doesn't that stress out the reindeer?" asked Billy Joe Bobby Jack.

"We've phased out the reindeer and brought in snowmobiles. Four Arctic Cats can do the job of nine reindeer, with less mess, and no red nose bulbs. I can't use reindeer anymore, anyway, since they were put on the endangered species list."

Krystal said, "Reindeer aren't endangered."

"Flying reindeer are."

BJBJ, whose family has been in the valley since Nick Wilson crawled over the Pass, said, "Since when can snowmobiles fly?"

"These are special machines, designed to meet the federal requirements for Yellowstone Park. Starting in 2006, snowmobiles in national parks must be silent, emit no emissions, and be able to fly."

Clyde is bitter about the snowmobile situation in Yellowstone. The air at the West Entrance got so murky employees started wearing gas masks, which the slednecks said was a publicity stunt; the air at the West Entrance in January, they said, is no worse than the air in the average cigar bar, where no one wears a gas mask. There was even talk of oxygen tanks for bison and wolves. A judge back East said, "No snowmobiles in the park till they can be made quieter."

Another judge in Cheyenne who considered himself local said, "If God didn't want noise in the wilderness he wouldn't have invented thunder. Bring in all the 'bilers you want."

The park people who actually live in Yellowstone said, "We don't want any." The judge in Cheyenne said the park employees were outsiders and he is pro-Wyoming, by which he meant pro-Wyoming business as opposed to pro-Wyoming plants, animals and people. He said, "You have to let them in."

Over the summer, the environmentalists, Park Service, snowmobilers and Republicans hammered out a compromise. They decided to cap the number of snowmobiles that can enter Yellowstone on any given day. I'm not sure why they called it a compromise because the cap is higher than the number of snowmobilers who came into the park back when it was unregulated. Maybe that's for the people who believe in Santa Claus to figure out.

"I make the elves fly the snowmobiles," Clyde said. "It saves on weight. That's why I have them living up the Gros Ventre River now."

Miss Periwinkle looked perplexed. This wasn't how she envisioned Santa Day in her curriculum planner. "But I don't understand. Why do the elves have to live on the Gros Ventre River?"

Clyde's jolly eyes twinkled, as if he'd been hoping someone would ask that question. "They live there to be near the Elf Refuge."

All nine toddlers pelted Clyde with sippy cups.

SUMMER 2005

Peter Pym came charging into my office last winter, all a-tizzy because he'd found the secret to marketing Jackson Hole.

Peter was waving a copy of *AARP: The Magazine* he claimed he stole from his acupuncturist's waiting room, but I know for a fact he gets them in the mail. If *AARP: The Magazine* really does have the highest circulation of any magazine in America, as it claims on the front cover, it also has the highest number of subscribers denying they read it.

Anyway, Peter thrust the magazine in my face and practically shouted. "I have found the way to insure our valley's future."

"You've reversed global warming?"

"Better. I now know how to sell Jackson Hole. Look." He showed me an article titled, "Five Countries Where the U.S. Is Not Hated." It was a rundown of all the spots in the world where American tourists can take vacations and not be treated like scum-sucking Norwegian wharf rats. For those few of you who may have missed the story, here is the list of foreign countries considered safe for the sensitive American to travel:

Northern Mariana Islands, Grenada, Belize, Andorra and Luxembourg.

"These are all nice destination resorts," I said, "but none of them strikes me as competition for Disney World."

"Not a country on the list bigger than Yellowstone," Peter said.

"I wonder what we did to hack off Southern Mariana Islands."

The royal family of Luxembourg generally vacations at a secret hilltop hotel overlooking Jackson Hole, and one of the princes told Delores that, in his country, whenever a citizen turns 18 they throw a party for him or her at the palace. Imagine that. I've been to Luxembourg. The tourist attraction is a bunch of cannons inside caves facing the mountain roads into the city. It's fascinating, but let's face it, two hours and you can pretty much say, "Done that."

"I firmly believe Americans are not comfortable spending their leisure time and money in a country where the waiters hiss as they enter a restaurant," Peter said.

"Not to mention the dollar tanking in Europe and Asia," I said. "Unless you love Andorra, this might be the summer to see America first."

"So here's my advertising campaign slogan." Peter made an imaginary headline with his hands. "Come to Jackson Hole — We Don't Hate You."

I pictured how Peter's slogan would look in a quarter-page display ad in *Field and Stream*. It reminded me of when we're on a trip and we see a motel with a sign out front that reads clean bathrooms. There's something about a place that feels the need to stress that as a positive. It makes me suspicious.

"How do you know it's true?" I asked.

"This is advertising. It doesn't have to be true."

"We'd have to get rid of all those bumper stickers that say, 'If it's tourist season, why can't we shoot them?' "

"My favorite is, 'You should have been here before people like you came here.' "

The truth is, the world over — not just in Wyoming — locals and tourists have what the self-help books call a co-dependent love/hate relationship. Tourists see locals as hicks out to fleece them of every dime possible. Locals see tourists as stupid. Consider how New Yorkers react with glee whenever one of their own sells some poor rural sap the Brooklyn Bridge. And Floridians with their baby-on-a-rope gator bait stories. Heck, in Paris lying to tourists is a spectator sport. Every time some city slicker buys into jackalopes or the Gros Ventre Slide or mogul storage units, we feel vastly superior.

The entire rubber tomahawk industry is built on out-of-towners paying cash for junk locals wouldn't touch with a stick. We are entertained to no end when they shell out $15 for earrings made out of shellacked elk poop. Back home, would these people pay the same amount for dog turd accessories? I don't think so. There's a store downtown making a killing on food that looks like excrement and excrement that looks like food. Only in America.

When I was a kid, a naturalist named Wally Butts worked up at Jenny Lake. Whenever tourists asked Wally where Jackson Hole was, he would take them out behind the museum there and show them a hole. One summer it was an under-construction outhouse. Another year, he showed them a chiseler hole. More than once, I saw families in winter coats and summer shorts taking photographs of the Jenny Lake chiseler hole. Lord knows what the Park Service would do to a ranger who pulled that stunt today.

Peter himself got his start in journalism after he told a tour group from Oklahoma the white stuff on the mountains was Styrofoam put there to break the falls of mountain climbers. They believed him, and he wrote a story about it. I'd like to see how Peter feels in Africa when they tell him the hippos are animatronic.

But it's not all locals making fun of tourists. The thing goes the other way, too.

"The very first tourists in the Yellowstone ecosystem managed to insult every local they met," Peter said.

"Are you fixing to tell me some ridiculous story that makes sense until I sit down later and think about it?"

"I'm fixing to tell you a true historical fact. Remember when Lewis and Clark came up the Missouri River?"

"I've heard about it."

"They stopped at each Indian village to trade beads and mirrors for horses and food."

"Cheating locals."

"Right, but before they moved on, they would ask the name of the next tribe off to the West. Those Indian tribes all called themselves The People. Or Human Beings, or just Us. How else do you expect people to look at themselves? But since the next tribe over was usually an enemy, or, at best, a rival, they gave Lewis and Clark the derogatory name. Blackfeet. Gros Ventre, which means Fat Belly. Nez Perce, which means Pierced Nose. Flathead. Dirt-Eaters. Even when explorers didn't insult a tribe by calling them Flatheads, they got the name wrong. They called the Raven tribe Crows and the Basket Weavers, Snakes."

"I see what you mean," I said. "It'd be like if the explorers came through here and asked, 'What people live over those mountains?' and we said, 'The ferocious Spud-for-Brains.' And they marched into Idaho Falls and said, 'All hail, you Spud-for-Brains.'"

"Or if they went through Rock Springs first on their way here, and after we all gathered in the Town Square to welcome them, the leader of the expedition said, 'We bring you greetings from the President of the United States to the Trust Fund Babies of Wyoming.'"

"Tourists say that all the time now," I said. "Except the part about greetings from the President. Jackson Hole needs a new image, something other than home of the Trust Fund Babies."

"Which brings us back to Come to Jackson Hole — We Don't Hate You."

"You think people paying $15 for shellacked elk poop earrings are going to believe that?"

"Don't scoff," Peter said. "If I sell enough elk poop this summer, next winter I'm taking the family to Andorra."

SUMMER 2006

Yosemite brought to you by Nike is more palatable than Nike State Park.
    – Krysti Argylian, general manager of Hill Holiday Advertising Agency

Roger Ramsey, Heather Heidi Walsowski-Smith, and I canoed across the north end of Jackson Lake and hiked up the Berry Creek drainage. Heather Heidi brought whole grain gnocchi and Roger carried a backpack full of Starbucks Frappuccinos. I brought along a copy of Walden by H.D. Thoreau. It's lighter than a Frappuccino.

"Did you hear the rumor?" Heather Heidi asked. "The Park is selling naming rights to the new visitor's center in Moose. It's going to Jaegermeister Center of the Tetons."

"I'm not sure they can use Tetons in the title," I said. "Delores told me Victoria's Secret has an exclusive to the T-word. The want to call it The Grand Tetons brought to you by the Miracle Secret Embroidered Satin Demi-Bra™.

"Viagra has a bid in on Old Faithful," Heather Heidi said.

We were on a roll now. "Golden Arches National Park."

"The Lincoln Lincoln Memorial."

If you haven't heard, our federal government, who once passed itself off as the Great White Father, has run out of money. In a panic, the administration based out of that scenic wonderland, Crawford, Texas, has suddenly realized the West is a check waiting to be cashed. They've ordered the Park Service to start a naming program whereby corporations who donate money are allowed to rename museums, trails, entrance gates, visitor centers, the law says they can even rename natural features, but the Department of Interior has said that even though it's legal and they can if they want, they are much too tasteful to rename a mountain after a product.

The administration says we should trust them on this.

I'll repeat that for those of you in denial — the administration says we should trust them not to take advantage of their own rules.

Heather Heidi stopped to drink a Frappuccino and explain the limits of the new policy. "They decided a corporation can't rename an entire park after itself, but they can use *Brought to you by* or *Official Beer of.*"

"Beer is okay?" asked Roger.

"Alcohol and tobacco are both encouraged. The Park Service can advertise things so bad for us that they aren't allowed on television."

For those of you who have never been up there, which is pretty much everyone, Berry Canyon is the nastiest hike in the Tetons. Besides the boat ride to the base of the canyon, the lack of a trail, the only verified poison ivy in northwest Wyoming, and more grizzly bear traffic than human, there's basically no reason to be there. So why did we go? I asked that myself.

"We're looking for two old mines," Roger said. "I have to prove they're here before I can restake the claim and privatize them."

Heather Heidi sat on a rock and pulled out her gnocchi. She'd brought a spork from McDonald's. Back in my day a spork was called a runcible spoon. "What would anyone mine in the Tetons?"

"The two old geezers who had the claims never told anyone what they were mining. Locals thought they were just up here, digging holes for the fun of it."

"Sounds like a Brokeback relationship," I said.

"Let's not go there," Heather Heidi said. "We're under orders, no Brokeback humor and nothing about vice presidents shooting lawyers."

"I'd rather talk about reality anyway," I said. "Why do you need to find these mines?"

"The Republicans rewrote the Mining Act of 1872. Anyone who can find a mining claim on public land can buy it. You don't even have to mine the land. I'm going to subdivide and put in a Marriott," Roger said.

"Is it a law yet, or only a bill," I asked.

"Only a bill now, but sooner or later the government is going to realize they can make a dent in the deficit by selling off the forests and parks. There's two plans out there now, with more on the way. Maurey already has a clearing out by Taggart Lake picked out. We're going to build a water park."

"At least the government is out to make a profit," Heather Heidi said. "I would think the Republicans would give the land to themselves."

"They're selling it for a thousand an acre," Roger said. "Teton County land is worth a million an acre. Do the math."

"That's why they want to rename Jackson Lake Sotheby's," I said.

This whole renaming thing sounds outlandish to me, although it's no worse than the old way we named new rape 'n' scrapes out West. Back in the old days, say the 1980s, whenever a natural feature was destroyed, we named the replacement after the person most likely to be devastated by the loss — Lake Powell, Colter Bay, Jim Bridger Power Plant.

Heather Heidi lifted her boot. "Is this grizzly bear poop?

This is grizzly bear poop. I'm not picnicking on gnocchi if there's grizzlies in the area. Bears love this stuff."

"It's coyote," Roger said.

"Coyotes don't eat berries."

I stayed on the subject of the column. "But how can you get people back here," I asked. "There's no road."

"That's why I have to move now, while Phil Hoffman is still Deputy Director of Interior."

"You mean Pave-the-Park Hoffman?"

"That's the guy. He rewrote the Park Service operations manual and threw out the old language about conservation and preservation. He wants to build four-lane highways in Yellowstone and new roads wherever anyone who can profit by them wants one. It's so bizarre a writer of satire can't make it funny by exaggeration."

Heather Heidi was amazed, which just shows you how naïve Heather Heidi is. "How can he get away with it?"

I always thought certain freedoms in America were absolute, but now I realize, if the votes are there, and this summer they are, there's nothing anyone can do to stop the American concepts from being wiped out. Maybe I'm as naïve as Heather Heidi.

Roger finished his Frappuccino and threw the empty bottle into the creek. "This fella Steve Martin, who's a big shot with the Park Service, he testified before Congress, and he said the more radical changes to the operating manual were 'inadvertent.' "

"Inadvertent means a mistake. It's a nice way to say 'Oops'."

"That's right. The parts of the new manual doing away with protecting plants and animals in the park system are only typos. They slipped through with no one knowing about them."

Heather Heidi waded out into the creek after Roger's bottle. She said, "That's weird, even coming from a politician."

"These Park Service administrators weren't politicians six years ago," Roger said. "They were stewards and scientists. At the worst, bureaucrats. But Hoffman has sent down word that anyone who disagrees with him publicly will be punished. Forced to choose between losing their pensions or making claims like this entire 138-page document is "inadvertent," the ones who can't afford to quit have decided to say "Oops."

The whole think made me so ill, I opened Walden and started reading.

Roger looked over my shoulder. "Did you know Snapple is the official drink of New York City. The bought the title for 166 million dollars. Pepsi bought San Diego. Coca Cola has Huntington Beach. Maybe we could make Frappuccino the official drink of the Teton Wilderness. I wonder how much we could make?"

"I wonder what Thoreau would think."

"Thoreau would have turned Walden Pond into Maxwell House for twenty bucks. He wasn't stupid, you know."

Heather Heidi said, "I'll stake my reputation on it. That is grizzly poop."

WINTER 2006

My five-year-old granddaughter, yearns for the good old days, back when she was three, or even two. "Remember when we used to watch *The Wiggles*?" she asked a couple of weeks ago. "That was so much fun"

Not that Krystal would be caught watching *The Wiggles* now. Our TV remote might as well be spot-welded to the Food Network—Rachael Ray and Giada De Laurentiis. I didn't even know what lemon zest was when I was five, much less the proper way to make it. And you should have heard the grief I got for fixing an omelet with olive oil that wasn't extra virgin. This from a child who still pronounces it "olemet." (Explaining the definition of *extra virgin* was challenging.)

I didn't think much of this nostalgia among the pre-K set until I went over to Clyde and Heather Heidi Walsowski-Smith's house the other night. They have two kids—Carly, sixteen, and Toby, six—and both were getting ready for flash-back parties. Carly was dressing up for something called a Millennium Ball, where everyone wears clothes that were popular on New Year's Eve, 1999. Her outfit included a belly-button-exposing top and low-rider pants.

I recall being shocked by '60s theme parties in the late '70s, but this is even more bizarre. This is high school kids dreaming of a better life seven years ago.

Wyoming was settled by pioneers facing forward. The past was dead and buried when we entered statehood. I can't imagine Jackson Holies holding an 1899 party in 1906. Now, we have a '49er Ball every winter, although so far as I can make out, nothing happened here in 1849. Even as late as 1949, Holies looked forward to a future with television, paved streets, and frozen TV dinners on metal trays you tossed in the trash after you were through eating. Folks didn't romanticize hanging a dead elk off the porch and hacking off slabs for supper. Women didn't feel closer to their inner spirit when they gave birth at home.

No one I know today looks forward to the future. This is especially true of kindergartners. Sure, they want to drive cars, date, and control their own credit cards, but they want that stuff right now. This minute. What they don't want is to grow up and have to pay for dental insurance and watch *Larry King Live* on CNN.

If we are absolutely forced to, most of us are willing to live in the present, although we'd rather be back when times were simpler and you could take a jelly-filled Krispy Kreme on an airplane. No one is in any hurry to rush into the future. Why is that? Why are there so many old-time photo studios and no Tomorrowlands in Jackson Hole? Why are 1950s diners popular and you never see those Buck Rogers knockoffs they had back in the '50s themselves? And why does the high school radio station never play anything newer than Bruce Springsteen's "Born To Run"?

Here's an interesting fact: More Americans go to museums than football games and NASCAR races combined. I didn't make that up, (As an aside, more people voted in the *American Idol* contest than in the last presidential election, but that's a whole other problem. Let's not even go there.)

You can't throw two or more thirty-whatevers in a room

without arguments breaking out over where the Silver Spur had their busboy housing and who blew both knees, shoulders, and hips in Corbett's Couloir in 1988. I've always wondered if towns with two or three continuous generations of locals worry about this stuff the way we do. I think the very transience of the people here makes them obsess with what was where when. I once met a girl who was a fifth generation Las Vegas, Nevada, native, and she didn't give a flying hoot where the Frontier Casino used to be. I suspect if we could find a fifth generation Holie, it would be the same story. He, or she, would say, "Who cares when the drive-in theater closed?" and everyone who'd been here only forty years would be aghast.

The reason this matters now is that we are coming into a pair of watershed winters. Last winter, the original tram still ran at the Village. Two winters from now, in theory, the new tram will take its place

I predict someday, much sooner than we dream now, locals will be divided between those who rode the original tram and locals who didn't. It sounds goofy today, but the time will come when old-tram skiers will be viewed as relics.

"Here's a picture of your Grandpa getting into the old tram, honey. Isn't it quaint?"

"Was that before the Civil War, or after, Mama?"

You may think this is impossible, but consider those who lived here even before the old tram was built, back when Teton Village was the Crystal Springs Girl Scout Ranch. No one imagined in 1966 that those who lived in the Hole pre-tram would one day be looked at as curiosities. *Ripley's Believe It Or Not* exhibits.

A better comparison might be what began on July 31, 1915. Before that day, automobiles were banned on Yellowstone roads. Through 1916, horse-drawn vehicles shared the road with cars, and by 1917 horse-drawn vehicles were banished. See, it's the same with the old tram. *Bing, bang, boom,* and you're ancient history. High school kids use you as a prom theme.

That brings up Toby's party. The kindergartners were having a July-in-November sock hop. They were dressing like they did in July, playing music they listened to last summer.

Toby said, "I remember those days. I was so happy back then."

Heather Heidi said, "You were six. Now, you're six and a half."

"Yes, but everything is different now."

In the words of my daughter, "I fwoad up."

SUMMER 2007

A couple years ago Randolph Proust, his lovely wife Chelsey, and their children Lester and Brittania camped at Lava Creek Campground in Yellowstone National Park. One hot afternoon, after lunch, a young cinnamon-colored black bear wandered into the campground and commenced to pop open various bear-proof trash receptacles. Randolph decided he would get a cute photo by smearing Sioux Bear honey across Lester's lips and chin.

"Think cuddly thoughts," Lester's mother said before sending the boy off to bond with nature's wonder.

The next day, when interviewed by the *Jackson Hole News and Guide* at the Lake Hotel Hospital, Mr. Proust said, "I didn't dream the Park Service would allow bears to roam freely if they weren't tame. My kids were raised on Berenstein Bears, Brother Bear, Bear in the Big Blue House. We came to Yellowstone to watch Yogi and Boo Boo steal picnic baskets."

Randolph's daughter clutched a Teddy Bear to her chest and cooed, "Winnie the Pooh bit off Lester's nose."

I thought of this story the other day when I ran into Roger Ramsey at Hard Drive Café where we was skimming back and forth across the internet, searching for happy-go-lucky dairy products.

"I know I've heard of Mr. Cheddar Curd." Roger's teeth gnashed in determination. "I just can't find him. Look at this. There's a Japanese anime starring the Tofu Twins. I can use that."

I ordered a half-caff, extra dry, soy vanilla cappuccino and came back to Roger and his computer. "Why are you Googling anthropomorphic cheese?" I asked.

"Because Maurey rented *Finding Nemo* for Scarlet and now she refuses to eat fish?"

"Maurey or Scarlet?"

"Scarlet. Maurey never would touch my trout." Maurey is Roger's wife. Scarlet Gilia is their six-year-old daughter. Roger calls her Scarlet and Maurey calls her Gilia. Maurey is an ovo-lacto vegetarian and Roger is a hunting guide. It's a marriage made on the second ring of hell.

"Maurey did it on purpose. All those cute little fish and crustaceans love their families and friends, and the evil humans want nothing more than to slaughter them. What does she think fish eat if not each other?"

"My theory is Disney characters live on fruit juice and Dove bars."

"Maurey's got Scarlet so she won't eat any food that sings and dances. It began with the stupid pig in *Charlotte's Web.* Then Benny the Bull from 'Dora the Explorer." She hasn't touched lamb since the damn thing followed Mary to school one day, and don't even get me started on Bambi."

This was interesting. I sat beside Roger and watched him fly from cartoon site to site. There were hundreds of them. "So Scarlet won't eat anything other than vegetables?"

"I nipped that in the bud. Went to the library and checked out a video called "Veggie-Tales." It's a bunch of Christian cucumbers and tomatoes and the like, teaching each other values. Scarlet sleeps with an artichoke heart now. She's been cutting out little velvet skirts and blouses for her carrots."

"How about apples and oranges?"

"I downloaded a Fruit of the Loom commercial. She's got nowhere left to turn except macaroni and cheese, and as soon as I find Mr. Cheddar Curd, I can put a stop to that."

I tried to see the logic in Roger's logic, but it zipped right over my head. "Why are you trying to starve your daughter to death?"

"I'm not trying to starve Scarlet. I'm showing her those idiot kids' shows have given everything a personality. I'll drive her back to Happy Meal burgers, like a normal child. Look at this site."

Roger stopped on the Boohbah Home Page. Boohbahs appear to be colorful amoebas with deep, creative emotions capable of expressing joy and sadness. "Better not show her that one," Roger said. "Lord knows what she might swear off."

He switched to Thomas the Tank Engine, which is a show about selfish, jealous, bitter trains who treat each other like human beings. "It's not just animals," Roger said. "There's a new show on Disney about talking screwdrivers. It's ripped off a PBS show where a front end loader cries when it doesn't get its way."

"Bob the Builder."

"This baloney didn't exist when I was a kid. You never saw the Three Stooges worrying about a cream pie's self-esteem."

"It's been going on forever," I said. "John Ruskin called it the Pathetic Fallacy."

"Somebody got rich selling pet rocks. I wouldn't call that pathetic."

"Back then pathetic didn't mean politics or sports or anything it's used for now. It meant empathetic. Ruskin had a peeve against angry clouds or majestic mountains. He said no matter how much it rains, the clouds are never angry. A cloud is nothing but a cloud. The river is not an old man. Tumbleweeds don't tumble because they are laid back."

"What's that got to do with forcing a rare rib eye down Scarlet's throat. I won't have a daughter so arrogant as to remove herself from the food chain."

"Ruskin's was a worthless complaint. Writers couldn't write without the Pathetic Fallacy. Humans couldn't be human. Ancient Greeks thought the sun, the moon, the oceans, even the earth itself were all gods who behaved like dysfunctional families. Even us modern types created God in man's image."

"Not the other way around?"

"Everything is personal to humans. That's what sets us apart from the monkeys."

Roger yelled, "Eureka!"

"You understand my philosophical treatise?"

"Chuck E. Cheese! She'll never eat macaroni and cheese again."

"Isn't Chuck E. a mouse?"

Roger leaned toward his computer and peered at Chuck. "Oh, yeah. Can't let her find this one. She already goes hysterical at the sight of D-Con."

"What if your plan doesn't work?" I asked Roger. "What if you're creating an anorexic? Girls today have enough neuroses without thinking their lunch is getting in touch with its inner pasta."

"I see the light," Roger said.

"You've discovered a way to use your brain?"

"I'll write a diet book. It'll make millions of dollars."

"Are these the same millions you made off of self-cleaning barbecue sauce?"

"Nobody ever lost a dime selling weight loss schemes. I'll call it the Yellowstone Diet. We'll turn South Beach into a Trivial Pursuit answer."

"Or Jeopardy question."

"Every woman in America will clamor for my DVDs and CD ROMS."

I finished my cappuccino and dug a finger into the bottom foam. "So, what are you selling exactly?"

"Tapes and movies of happy food groups. Living lunch. Whenever a woman puts anything whatsoever in her mouth, we'll convince her she's murdering Tinkerbell."

"Or whoever."

Roger grinned. "Whomever."

WINTER 2007

Kelly Walsowski-Smith is suing Charisse Free Spirit, the owner of the Snooty Coyote Espresso Bar and Day Spa, because she purchases a Jackson Hole Mountain Pass for her winter employees, and Kelly doesn't ski.

"Those passes cost you almost two thousand bucks apiece," Kelly said. "I want two thousand dollars cash, so I'm getting paid the same as everyone else."

Charisse looked up from unpacking the seaweed wraps used in her Mount Moran facials. She guarantees her facial treatments when taken with a lomilomi massage and a double decaf soy macchiato to bring inner peace or your money back. Charisse is so calm herself she's thinking of changing her name again, to Tranquility. Her original name was Cherry Dumbledore.

Charisse centered her consciousness and closed her eyes for a five-count single-nostril inhalation. Reopening her eyes, she said, "Fat chance."

"But it's not fair. Just because I don't ski, you're punishing me."

Charisse exhaled from the other nostril. "Had I known you don't downhill, I never would have hired you. What if my customers find out my employees are not among the vibrant set? You are a wicked child for not exposing your faults when you asked for the job."

"It wasn't on the application."

"I was against the Don't Ask, Don't Tell policy right from the beginning, when the county commissioners passed the law. I knew you flatland riffraff would come crawling out of the closet."

"Cherry, you're living in the Reagan years. Nobody cares what sports their masseuses partake of anymore. I'm proud I don't ski."

"Why don't you go back to Kansas, or wherever you and Toto came from?"

"I was born in Jackson," Kelly said. "I don't have to justify my existence. Like you."

Charisse clapped her hands sharply to expel the bad vibrations from the room. "The bonus is a ski pass. I provide it for my workers out of the purity of my soul. I don't care whether you use it or not."

"You give them a pass because there's a thousand vacant jobs in this valley right now. You should be buying each of us a new Prius, for not leaving you for the coal-bed methane patch."

Kelly's dream is to paint bank-check backgrounds. When she told her mother, Heather Heidi, about her aspirations, H.H. felt like she'd swallowed a brick.

"What are bank-check backgrounds?" Heather Heidi asked, in disbelief.

"The paintings behind the words and bar code on a check. The universal art form. You have the Baby Barnyard Buddies on yours. The cuddly-four series. Dad has Scenes from National Parks. Practically everyone carries personal-check paintings. Imagine creating a work of art that millions and millions of bank customers use every day. For two thousand dollars, I can take a course on CheckArt.net."

That's why Kelly is desperate for two thousand dollars,

almost exactly the price of the ski pass Charisse is providing as incentive to prospective employees.

"The Free Spirits own Wilson. You can't sue them," Heather Heidi said.

"Watch me," Kelly said.

"Who do you think you are?"

Kelly drew herself up to her five-foot-two tallest. "I am an artist."

Five years ago, locals who didn't downhill ski kept their mouths shut. Friends and co-workers would gush over powder and moguls and lines through the trees, and we non-skiers would nod our heads knowingly, as if we understood every nuance. Made me feel like a psychiatrist.

There was even a secret club — NIDS (No, I Don't Ski) — that met in the basement of the Forest Service rec hall, every other Tuesday, to eat cheese blintzes and discuss topics other than winter sports. The club was secret because of the unwritten town ordinance against expressing views about art or literature. Or even cheese blintz recipes. Having a family member who didn't downhill was a dark curse that oft times led to public shunning at the post office.

So, what happened, you may well ask. What event came to pass that brought the non-skiers out of the basement and lifted them into the sunlight? What happened was this: A bunch of people — millionaires and billionaires, mostly — came together and built the Center for the Arts. The CFA. Suddenly, there was a sanctuary for artists, dancers, musicians, actors, even writers. Now there was something to do that had nothing to do with freezing your feet. Even better, there was a nonalcohol, non-television alternative after dark. Folks stepped forward, proudly, before their community, and shouted, *"I am into ceramics!"* Or, *"I can Photoshop. Can you?"*

The doors of civility were kicked open and once you turn loose a tsunami of artistes, there's no stopping them. Five years ago, you had downhill skiing or you had hiding your interests, alone, feeling like the freak of Wyoming. Now we have a third choice—creativity.

Heather Heidi Walsowski-Smith has a job now, guiding walking tours of the new parking garage there across from the post office. The garage is four or five stories high, depending on how you count stories. The roof opens up on a dynamite view of the town and surrounding mountains. It's rapidly turning into the most popular sunset watching site in the area.

The garage is popular for any number of reasons — skateboard park, indoor exercise incline, submarine races — but none of these involve the intended use. The evening Heather Heidi escorted her husband Clyde and me up to the roof, there were four cars parked in the garage, and two of them had Day-Glo Abandoned Vehicle stickers on the window.

"Wyomingites are not parking garage savvy," Heather Heidi said. "They drive in here and turn claustrophobic. Or lost. They lead other cars into dead end cubbyholes, go in the exits and out the entrances. We scraped off two bike racks and a kayak yesterday."

Clyde said, "Wait till next winter when the ice adds a couple of inches height to the road, and people who have been zipping in and out for months suddenly start turning their trucks into convertibles." Clyde hates the new parking structure. A fair number of old-timers who moved here for small town ambiance resent the parking structure. The call it the Bismarck, because of its resemblance to a battleship.

Heather Heidi went into her Chamber of Commerce spiel: "At a cost of 10.5 million dollars, the structure is 51 feet high and creates 280 new parking spaces."

My cell phone has a calculator function. It didn't take long to figure. "That's $37,500 per space."

H.H. said, "We should outfit them with parking meters."

"The place we need parking meters is around the square," I said. "We could install those high-tech weenie meters that take credit cards, like they have in Scottsdale. It would be a total tourist tax. No locals park on the square anyway."

"The West wasn't won with paid parking," Clyde said.

The parking meter issue is splitting the town in a bitter battle, turning father against son and brother against brother, the way abortion and worm fishing used to. The pro-parking meter people, like me, point out the huge income generated from folks other than us. The anti-parking meter people, like Clyde, refuse to give the government money for anything that was free when there were in high school. The majority of the anti-meter party are also anti-parking garage.

Heather Heidi said, "The town fathers are afraid tourists will be put off by parking meters."

I said, "Let's picture a family in Frostbite Falls, Minnesota, torn between vacationing in the Tetons or Banff. Can you honestly see the father of the family saying, 'We have to skip Jackson Hole. They have parking meters'?"

Clyde looked off the garage toward the east, with its magnificent view of the Center of the Arts. "Any truth to the rumor they're going to use the capital facilities tax to build a sky bridge from here, over the Western Motel, and into the Center for the Arts?"

Heather Heidi said, "I'm not allowed to comment on that."

"Folks would finally park here if they did. We could put a coffee kiosk in it, like the sky bridge in Mesquite."

Heather Heidi said, "I can confirm the plan to place a web cam on the roof, with a view of Teton Pass."

Clyde snorted derision. Web cams are another of Clyde's pet peeves. Clyde has more pet peeves than Raisin Bran has raisins.

"My daughter is at home this moment," Clyde said, "watching a web cam of the South Pole. Jackson kids are surrounded by a million acres of nature, and the closest they come to wild places is looking at them on a computer."

Which is true — because most parents secretly prefer it that way. We pretend we don't, but a kid in a dark room peering into a flickering computer screen hardly ever gets ticks, skin cancer, kidnapped, eaten by a mountain lion, drunk, or pregnant. They don't fall off cliffs. Don't die in car wrecks. For every parent laying grief on a child for not playing outside, there are four who are glad their kid isn't.

At five, my daughter knew an octopus has three hearts, because she'd helped dissect one. She could diagram the social structure of a wolf pack, but she'd never walked barefoot through the grass. Her generation knows more about nature with less first-hand knowledge than any generation in history. They can't go outside without lathering on enough sunscreen to black out London during the Blitz. They can't play in their own front yard without adult supervision. My daughter still isn't allowed to walk to Taggart Lake alone, because the forest is full of bears and sex offenders.

"I read where by 2010 more people will be watching Old Faithful on the web cam than in person," Clyde said. "Yellowstone will be too uncomfortable, dangerous, and expensive to actually visit."

"With a web cam, there's no point," I said.

"Besides," Heather Heidi said, "everyone knows Old Faithful is fake. If you're going to watch man-made spew, I'd rather watch the Bellagio Fountains. They dance to Frank Sinatra."

Clyde nodded knowingly, but I was shocked. "I didn't know Old Faithful is fake."

"You are so not savvy," Clyde said. "Old Faithful is no more real than the Tooth Fairy, or the Compassionate Conservative."

Heather Heidi said, "Yellowstone had an earthquake in April of 1998, dried up Old Faithful and the entire Upper Geyser Basin, right in the middle of remodeling the Snow Lodge. The Park Service laid in pipes, real quick like. A GS-9 up in the garret of the Inn turns it on and off now. You must be the last local to find out the truth."

I thought about my Mother's Day trip to Old Faithful in May. The geyser did look more like a broken lawn sprinkler than the Old Faithful of my youth. "Can you prove that?" I asked.

"Sure," Heather Heidi said. "I can prove it by the *If it must be, it is* Law of Nature."

"I haven't heard of that one."

"Let's say you've spent over a billion dollars developing the single most famous tourist attraction in the entire world — three hotels, a museum, two gas stations, curio shops the size of a mall..."

"I get it."

"Now, let's imagine the tourist attraction dries up."

"I can picture that too."

"Would you, as the developer, say 'Oops,' and walk away from your billion dollar investment, or would you run a pipe across the meadow and keep the dream alive?"

"You are right. I would fake it."

"And, how do you know this hasn't already happened?"

I considered the odds. "It hasn't because the American government would never play tricks on its people."

Heather Heidi giggled. "There is a difference between not savvy and stupid, Tim. You just crossed the line."

Heather Heidi Walsowski-Smith came charging into the library where I was measuring letters to the editor with a tape measure I got free from public radio. Instead of launching into complaints about the weather, which is how Heather Heidi usually opens conversations, she said, "Give me your cell phone."

"This is the library. You can't phone chat here."

"I'm in the midst of an emergency. A matter of life and death."

I held onto my phone. Heather Heidi considers an empty toilet paper dispenser an emergency. She once called 911 over a bee in her car. "What's wrong with your phone?"

"Crimestoppers has blocked my number. Whenever a car runs a crosswalk while I'm in it, I call Crimestoppers and the last time the woman there was rude. She threatened to withdraw my right to police protection."

"I've never heard of Crimestoppers blocking a number. How often do you call them?"

"Every time I almost get killed crossing the street. It happened just now, with a truck from Idaho. The spud-for-brains sped up when he saw me step off the curb."

"Idaho truck drivers think crosswalks are cattle guards."

"Clyde says my dying words will be, 'I had the right of way, you jerk.' Why are you measuring the newspaper?"

"I'm counting inches of letters to the editor for my master's thesis. Jackson Hole has the highest per capita rate of writers of letters to the editor in the nation. We're over 12 times the average as established by a blogger from Pennsylvania who tracks these things."

"I've written three on crosswalk sanctity myself. And one against downhill skiers on cell phones."

"Half the valley has written letters to the editor about skiers on cell phones. There's a group in favor of shooting the phones, right off the skier's ear muff."

"Those hands-free talkers are the ones who scare me. It's so bad now, I can't tell the psychotics from the Yuppie scum."

Heather Heidi grabbed my paper. She made me lose my measuring spot. I would have to start over.

"Let's check out this week's hot topics," she said. Her finger ran down the columns of letters. "Here's a fella has invented a car that runs on elk pellets. Says it will solve America's energy crisis."

"There's another one demands we stop feeding elk. They clash."

Heather Heidi ignored me, as usual. "A woman from Malibu wants radiant heat under the pavement on Teton Pass. And here's a kid says you shouldn't use bear repellant the same way as mosquito repellant. He wants a warning on the cans."

"I wonder how he figured it out."

"The world's angriest man is outraged by the lack of ATMs in the back country. This clown claims proof of Tralfamadorians living in Mount Moran. It's Adopt-A-Chiseler Month. Two against global warming and one in favor. This character wants to rename the Jackson Hole Airport after Dick Cheney."

"That would solve the overcrowding problem."

"Carve Hannah Montana's head on Jackson Peak. Bring the

Winter Olympics to Wilson. Dynamite the Snake River bridges. A law against tunnels leading to condominiums."

"There's even one advocating a moratorium on letters to the editor."

"What the newspaper needs is a flake filter."

"Heck, yes, everyone agrees on that," I said, "but no one can agree on who should get the job. I wouldn't let right-wing born again vegans publish their opinions; you would cut off men who drive SUVs. Clyde thinks the government should confiscate e-mail accounts from any woman who doesn't shave her legs weekly."

"One man's flake is another man's granola."

"That's a fairly stupid yet true way to word it."

Heather Heidi continued to read letters. Counting long letters called Guest Shots, they made up 90% of the front section. "So what's the thesis of your master's thesis? You must have a theory since you are nothing if not a damn font of crackpot ideas."

"As a matter of fact, I do have a theory."

"I knew it."

"Residents of Duncan, Oklahoma, or Panama City, Florida, feel no empowerment when it comes to local environment. They are powerless."

"Remember when the town changed the Christmas lights in the Square from colored to white. The mayor got death threats."

"That wouldn't happen in Oklahoma."

"And you're bound to explain why."

"It's because people in the crowded time zones have no sense of control over their lives. They're stuck, whereas folks here tend to be black sheep from stable families gone to the wilderness to carve out purposeful lives. We've also had ourselves a veritable influx of filthy rich folks lately. Filthy rich folks think they deserve a say in what goes on. Take for example, the diapers on stagecoach horses controversy."

"I thought we'd break into class warfare."

"People who live with actual gangs, aggressive crackheads, strip malls, and professional politicians feel no control, so they keep their mouths shut and do whatever it takes to make the next mortgage payment. It's the difference between riding a horse and taking the subway."

"They both smell like old pee?"

"They're both transportation, but the choices of destination vary considerably."

"Here's a letter that might cure America's malaise," Heather Heidi said. "It's from Loretta O'Talley."

"Loretta writes letters every week. She needs her own private spam filter."

"Listen." Heather Heidi cleared her throat.

Dear Editor: What's all this fuss about Affordable Hosing? Don't we get enough snow directly from God Hisownself? Last winter the snow on both sides of my driveway was Okla-hanolooshi. (An Arapaho word meaning armpit high to a tall Shoshone.)

The last thing we need is to manufacture more snow so kids can snowboard in September. Kids should be in school in September. And, let me make this clear, snow from hoses is never affordable. What with the Canadian Cartel, it can go over a dollar a winejet. (A fluctuating measure of weight based on the number of aluminum cans you have to collect and sell at recycling to buy a bottle of Blue Nun. The rise and fall of this unit of measurement is watched as closely as the stock market by certain ski bums.)

We simply cannot afford hosing in Teton County. People who want hosing should move to Southern California, or better yet — Greece. My niece says housing in Greece is cheap.

Heather Heidi looked up at me. "I have no idea what that means."

"I don't want to know."

"Maybe Loretta O'Talley is lonely and frustrated."

"My research has found many compulsive writers of letters to the editor have no one who will listen to them."

"The town council should buy Loretta a cat."

SUMMER 2009

T his one brought in a death threat.

Clyde Walsowski-Smith had a dream. He aspired to be the first American to carry a semi-automatic assault weapon into Taggart Lake in Grand Teton National Park, and this winter — thanks to an Interior Department ruling in the last days of the Bush Administration — Clyde got his chance. He called me in late February, the first day the temperature broke twenty degrees.

Clyde said, "The time to make history is nigh."

"Can't we make history in June. I'd rather have our feet on the ground if you're armed."

"The way this country works some idiot judge is likely to change the rules by summer. This is our window of firearms opportunity."

Making gun history wasn't high on my personal to-do list, but I figured it would be a hoot to see how recreational cross-country skiers reacted when faced with a howling commando.

Would they cheer us on as patriots or hide their women and children?

Clyde picked me up wearing a camo pattern called Ghilli-Flage. Made him look like Bigfoot enshrouded in poison ivy. He said, "Let's go exercise our Second Amendment rights."

"I wish there was a right to drink another cup of coffee. That would be freedom on parade."

"Democrats drink coffee," Clyde said. "Sportsmen drink beer. Let's have one."

After his first Blue Ribbon of the day, Clyde gave me a lesson in civics. He stopped his Yukon at the Grand Teton pullout north of town, then he stood by the welcome sign with his rifle — a Bushmaster AR-15, for those of you who care — in his right hand and a large dress-size plastic bag from Coldwater Creek in his left.

"This side of the line is Wyoming," Clyde said. "My weapon must be clearly visible." As he crossed the park boundary, he slid the Bushmaster into the Coldwater Creek bag. "This side of the line is national park. To be legal here, the gun must be concealed from view."

"Why is that?" I asked.

"Because the Department of Interior hates the state of Wyoming," Clyde said, "And vice versa."

"I always tell my daughter that what's legal is the same as what's right and not wrong. How am I supposed to explain this to her?"

"I wouldn't bother. Get in the truck."

In the Cottonwood Creek parking lot, Clyde discovered we couldn't ride snowmachines into Taggart Lake. We would actually have to snowshoe a couple of miles. He said, "What's the use of it being legal to carry a gun someplace you can't drive to?"

"There's nothing in the Bill of Rights about freedom to drive a snowmobile anywhere you damn well please," I said.

Clyde sat on his tailgate and lit a Cuban cigar. "There would have been if the Founding Fathers had known about Arctic Cats."

Several skiers in environmentally correct L.L. Bean-wear passed by. They frowned at the cigar smoke, then frowned even more at the AR-15, clearly visible in the Coldwater Creek bag. This woman with a hundred dollar Lycra pants, bear bells, and a hands-free Blackberry gave us grief.

She said, "You can carry a gun but the plants, animals, and rocks are protected. What are you planning to shoot?"

Clyde blew smoke at her. "Wolf lovers and tofu queens."

The woman said, "You are disgusting."

Clyde said, "You must be from California."

After she left in a huff, I said, "She's right, Clyde. You can haul a gun up the trail, but you can't shoot it. What's the point?"

"You don't have principles, so you wouldn't understand."

"And the principle is no one can deny you your gun, anywhere, anytime."

Clyde nodded and fell back on bumper sticker gibberish. "The West wasn't won with a registered gun."

"Actually, it was, Clyde. Tombstone, Dodge City — all those Western frontier towns had laws where the cowboys had to check their guns at the Sheriff's office."

Clyde growled. "They'd never get away with that now."

"That's what I'm trying to tell you, meathead. Laws are more pro-gun-nut now than they've ever been in American history. Did you read about the Girl Scout Cookie Law the Wyoming Legislature passed last year?"

"I prefer to call it the No Retreat Law."

"If anyone enters your house — in Wyoming — without an invitation, you can legally kill them dead — no consequences."

"You say that like it's a bad thing."

"I wouldn't want to be a politician going door-to-door. For the killing to be legal, they have to cross the threshold, but once you blow their brains out it's just the dead guy's word against the shooter as to the invite."

Clyde arranged his camo get-up around the tailgate so he looked more like Swamp Thing than Bigfoot. "I daresay you exaggerate. No one's wasted a Girl Scout selling cookies yet."

"But they could. Same with Jehovah's Witnesses, cable guys, phone installers, census takers. Pretty soon, no one will ever knock on a door in Wyoming. We'll be totally isolated."

"Let's walk." We snowshoed while Clyde thought. It wasn't long before we were post holing in knee-deep powder. After twenty yards of this, Clyde stopped again and said, "I can live with that. The Constitution is more sacred than the life of a meter reader. Anyone who thinks different isn't American."

I couldn't help but wonder if Clyde had any limits when it came to gun rights. "What's the NRA's position on web cam hunting?" I asked.

"We say it's none of the government's business whether you hunt indoors or outside."

The Wyoming Legislature passed a law against web cam hunting this winter. At first, I thought it was a joke, like something I might make up for a column, but Clyde showed me the web site — Live-Shot.com. I was able to watch, although I couldn't pull the trigger. The hunter paid $1,500 for that privilege. There's crosshairs and a gun barrel. It looked like a video game until I realized the deer were real.

"Watch this," Clyde said. We were in McDonald's, using the free wifi. On the screen, a deer grazed along a chicken wire fence. "They're hazed in a yard," Clyde said, "so the hunter doesn't have to watch the camera for hours."

"Where is this?" I asked.

"Where do you think?"

"Texas." Texas's gun laws are even looser than Wyoming's. Basically, anyone can shoot anyone they please in Texas. You can claim future self-defense.

On the screen, a deer walked through the crosshairs and

BLAM! some fanatic sitting in his pajamas in Miami or L.A. or someplace else cozy blasted himself a noble animal. The deer pitched over and went down like a sack of meat falling off a truck.

The camera view was cut off. "Why'd they stop the picture?" I asked.

"They don't want the sportsman to overexcite himself and gut shoot the game management specialist."

"That is?"

"The skinner. They Fed Ex the head to whoever paid to kill him."

So, the McDonald's flashback came to an end and we found ourselves back on the trail to Taggart Lake, and I'm asking Clyde about the NRA stance on killing by web cam.

"When the Wyoming Legislature voted to ban web cam hunting, four Republicans voted against the bill," Clyde said.

"They must be heroes to the gun lobby. You think the NRA will go after everyone else?"

"It's the American way," Clyde said. "Label anyone who disagrees with you as a friend of terror."

"Texas is the only state where that works anymore."

Clyde puffed his cigar. "I'm thinking to move to Texas."

WINTER 2009

D elores Pym and I sat in McDonald's last summer, using their free Wi-Fi to watch the Old Faithful webcam. I prefer Old Faithful in person, while Delores doesn't see the difference between web and live. What I preferred didn't really matter, though, because road construction had basically cut Yellowstone off from the rest of Wyoming. It was easier to reach Paris than West Thumb.

Delores said, "I got my Facebook, MySpace, Twitter, texting, IM, three e-mail accounts, and Skype all right here." She adjusted the camera on her laptop. "Plus French fries. A person can lead a rich, creative social life and never step out of Mickey D's."

I gave her the benefit of my wisdom. "People who live with no regard for weather systems shrivel up inside. Spiritually speaking. That's why folks from the coastal time zones have no souls."

On the computer screen, the crowd was building to a Lycra-clad mob. The modern day explorer can tell just how long before a geyser emission based on the size and attention span of the crowd. I figured we had eight minutes.

"Why are you watching Old Faithful, anyway, if you've lost touch with nature?"

Delores said, "I'm not watching the geyser. I'm waiting for my daughter to show up. Cora Ann told me she was on her way to Yellowstone with girl chums, but I don't buy it. If she shows her face with that little punk Conrad Bierney I'm going to put a Breathalyzer ignition on her Prius, like they give the DUI freaks. Conrad is a known corrupter of underage females."

"Isn't that draconian, treating her like a criminal when she's not one?"

The cam view refreshed, revealing an even-larger crowd. Approximately 40 percent held ice cream, 25 percent specialized coffee drinks. Three prepubescent boys beat the snot out of a fourth while their parents bent over cell phones.

"Draconian is another word for good parenting," Delores said. "Soon, every teenager will have to blow clean air before they can start their car. I foresee a day when Breathalyzer ignitions will be as standard as seat belts."

Old Faithful gave a false eruption. Cameras went up like swords at a military parade. The few without cameras pointed fingers. I've been to Old Faithful so many times, I could hear a thousand husbands saying, "Was that it?"

Delores pulled her eyes from the screen to look at me. "What are you doing here? I thought chain fast food went against your chakras or feng shui or whatever."

"Not if I buy a parfait. *Parfait* is a French word and French food cancels karmic imbalance. Besides, I'm celebrating fifty years of living in Jackson Hole. Metaphorically speaking, McDonald's seemed the perfect place to mark the anniversary."

"Why must everything be a symbol? Don't you ever just eat?"

"Look who views life though a webcam."

"I'll bet everyone you tell about your fifty-year marker gives you a wink and a nudge and says, 'Guess you've seen some changes in the valley, huh? Huh?'"

She was right on that. It's as if people think Jackson pulled a reverse butterfly to cocoon to wormy-thing transformation. Far as I can recall, the town itself never was a butterfly.

"Any population that grows from 2,500 to 25,000 with the tourists going from 200,000 to over four million is going to look back at the past as the good old days. That's simple. What knocks me upside the head is the changes in nature her ownself."

"And you're about to tell me what those changes are."

"Mostly, it's in the *ick* factor animals. In the sixties, we never saw a tick or a leech. We had no vultures. Practically no snakes. The valley's first black widow spider was discovered just last month. But when I was a kid I saw almost as many rabbits as chiselers. And fireflies. When was the last time you saw a firefly?"

"I think you're suffering from false memory syndrome on that one."

"When I was young Otter Glacier had legs and Skillet Glacier had a handle."

"God, I hope this won't turn political."

"Yellowstone burned. Jackson Drug closed. The scientists even ripped three feet off the official height of the Grand. Continuity is dead. Everything has changed except the Cowboy Bar."

Delores switched the webcam to the Town Square, where we watched two old ladies in blue hair and red tennis shoes trying to pry antlers off one of the arches. Then she switched to the Ferris wheel on the Santa Monica pier. It was all the same to her.

"You think the rest of America wastes as much energy on nostalgic trivia as we do in Jackson Hole?" Delores asked. "It only takes six months before our invaders are old-timers, comparing notes on what used to be where and wasn't it better when."

"My daughter started at four years old, yearning the simple

days of yore when she was two."

Delores glanced at me as she switched the computer back to Old Faithful. "Your daughter was born in Advanced Placement."

"Speaking of daughters, there's yours."

A group of teenage girls in what appeared to be Bangkok hooker-wear entered the picture. Cora Ann was riding on the shoulders of a kid wearing a wife-beater and shorts that showed his crack. He had enough tattoos to get a job on the rubber duck races at a county fair. Cora Ann's arms were upraised, as if she'd just won a snowboard medal.

"I'll ground her for life," Delores said.

I ignored her problems, stuck in my own personal obsession with the past. "Tony Deloney once told me nothing good has happened in Jackson since 1922."

"I read where the 1890s homesteaders loathed the wave that came in the 1920s. Called them Better-Than-Thous. The 1890s crowd were basically hippies of the slovenly variety and the twenties bunch wanted churches and indoor potties."

"This valley has been living the *Shane* story over and over since the Ice Age. Cattlemen drove out the trappers who cleared out the Indians. Sodbusters fenced off the cattlemen. Ski area granola snappers drove out the townies only to be displaced themselves by developers who sold the land to millionaires who lost it to billionaires. Only thing you can count on in Jackson Hole is the longer you live here the less people you're going to know."

"My daughter's riding an Ultimate Fighting Championship wannabe and you expect my heart to bleed 'cause after fifty years you don't know anyone when you walk in the grocery store?"

Torn between cynicism and self-pity, I opted for sarcasm with a hint of underlying pathos. "That's why I came to McDonald's to celebrate a half century in Jackson Hole. This right here"—I pointed to my mass-produced parfait in a plastic cup—"is our blessed valley."

SUMMER 2010

Somebody's gonna have to start talking about these things."
— Bullwinkle

I'm not certain how Clyde Walsowski-Smith first heard about moose cheese. I suspect the information came from one of his horn hunting buddies, those guys looking to get rich off nature's leftovers. However Clyde got the word, when told the stuff sells for $500 a pound, he decided he absolutely had to milk a moose.

"You squeeze out a gallon a session," he fairly shouted at me. "That's seven pounds a day times 500 a pound."

I considered his level of seriousness. "Does a pound of milk translate into a pound of cheese?"

"It only makes sense. I even found a market — a Beverly Hills cheese shop, south of Little Santa Monica Boulevard. Those movie people will pay whatever it costs to buy a product normal people can't afford."

"You think moose cheese tastes like $500 a pound?"

"Taste doesn't mean squat in the rare food business. Exclusivity is the only factor. Nobody would touch caviar if McDonalds gave it away in a Happy Meal."

Three of us signed up for the mission — Clyde, Roger Ramsey, and me. At the last moment, Roger's girlfriend Maurey decided to come along.

"I'll record the historic feat on my I Phone," she said. "We'll post Clyde's death on You Tube and make him famous for a day."

Clyde said, "Milking moose never killed anyone. All you need is rubber gloves and a bucket."

As this had the makings of a fiasco, I went home and researched. I mean, we're not fools in Wyoming. There's a point where bravery and stupidity overlap, and the brave person is the one who has done his research.

Here's the rundown: Currently, there are two commercial moose milk operations. The first, in Russia, only supplies milk for medicinal purposes. Moose milk — 12% fat, 12% protein, 21.5% solids such as selenium and zinc — is served at your upscale sanatoriums and given to kids with gastroenterological diseases. Think organic Milk of Magnesia.

All the free market moose cheese in the world — before Clyde anyway — comes from three moose named Gullen, Haelga, and Juna, who live on a farm near Bjurshelm, Sweden. The fact that the moose have names makes me suspect they might be domesticated. I mentioned this to Clyde.

He came back with the pithiest line he could think up, considering he's a man without insurance. "So what?"

My other qualm surfaced when I read that moose only produce milk the first three months after they've given birth.

"Female moose with calves tend to irritability," I said. "Even more so than the average bull in rut."

Roger had an answer, of course. "They only get pissed when you threaten the calf and we're not milking the calf. We're milking the mother. What's she going to do — call Bob Barker?"

The moose Clyde chose to milk live in the willow flats between Jackson Lake Lodge and Jackson Lake. He knew one would be simple to find there because the Park Service herds a few exhibition moose within sight of the back deck at the lodge for wealthy tourists with expensive camera get-ups. I advanced the idea that the rangers might object to public moose abuse.

Clyde barked. "There's no law against milking a moose in the Park."

"There's no law against giving a grizzly bear a root canal either but that doesn't make it a dandy thing to do. The rangers fly off the handle when idiots die in front of tourists."

Clyde outfitted the men with horses. Mine was an appaloosa named Nellie, just like the horse Little Joe rode in *Bonanza*. Clyde promised she'd been trained to haul out-of-state children so I was safe as Grandpa on a Barcalounger.

I patted her spotted face. "Has she been trained in roping moose?"

"It's an instinct with appaloosa. The Spaniards bred them for the bull ring," which may make sense to you but I missed the connection. Maurey hiked in on foot, for filming flexibility. She had no intention of approaching an actual wild animal.

She said, "If she stomps your head, don't expect me to say 'Tut, tut, poor baby.' You guys deserve whatever happens."

Roger said, "Thanks, honey."

Clyde brought his pistol because that's legal now, in Grand Teton Park, and he does enjoy flaunting his rights.

"You planning to shoot a moose in front of that gang of hedge fund babies at Jackson Lake Lodge?" Maurey asked.

"If I'm in imminent danger it will be legal as drinking beer."

"If a jerk yanks a moose's tit I'd say imminent danger is a guarantee."

As any cowboy knows, the secret to roping a wild beast bigger than a badger is triangulation. It takes three ropes and three horses who can back up quick and stand steady. The last Saturday afternoon in June found Roger, Clyde, and me triangulating a mama moose in the willows a hundred yards out from

Jackson Lake Lodge's picture windows. Maurey stood off to the rear, learning how to use her phone's zoom feature.

The moose eyed us as she chewed something wet, green, and stringy, not so much nervous as watchful. The calf huddled close to her side, more hungry than scared. National Park moose have no inborn fear of humans.

Clyde zipped in first, twirling his lariat and charging straight at her. He tossed the loop over her head where it slipped down onto her neck and then he took off south. The mother moose reared up on her hind legs in a Hi Ho Silver maneuver. Folks back on the lodge deck reached for their cell phones. That's the American way to handle a crisis nowadays. Grab a phone, first.

Clyde hollered at Roger and me to get our ropes on her and sooner beat the heck out of later. Roger went in crouched low in the saddle. He dropped his loop to the ground, the moose came down with her right front hoof encircled, and Roger's horse ran north with speed.

That left me and I've never roped so much as a fence post, but with them pulling hard in opposite ways, I got off Nellie and waded into the fray. I had to round the calf, which seemed to hack off the mother even more than two ropes yanking on her.

"You sure this is how they do in Sweden?" I asked.

Clyde said, "Get a noose on her while she's still calm."

I threw my loop just as the moose reared upright again and, by some miracle that proves God vacations in Wyoming, I snagged her by that dangly thing that hung down from her throat. On a turkey, it's called a wattle. I don't know what it's called on a moose, except on males they're big and on females they're little. I yanked like setting the hook on a trout and ran hell bent for Nellie. The moose charged after me. Have you ever seen a dog on a clothesline lead chase a cat? She went from full throttle to flipped over in a heartbeat, then she bounced back upright while I mounted Nellie and wrapped the rope snug around her saddle horn.

Maurey called, "I missed your throw, Tim. You mind doing it again?"

I glanced over at the Lodge deck in time to see the arrival of a pair of Park rangers. Numerous witnesses pointed my way. The rangers appeared to have lost their sense of humor.

Clyde hollered at Maurey. "I'm busy here. You'll have to take the bucket and milk her."

Maurey looked from Clyde to the calf to our audience on their cell phones to the bucket at her feet and back to the moose whose eyes bulged to the point where they threatened to pop out and splatter somebody.

Maurey said, "Like hell. I'm no milkmaid."

Clyde said something ugly about women's lib, burnt bras, and braided armpits, then he dismounted, stomped over to Maurey, snatched up the bucket and walked toward the moose, only by now I wouldn't call Clyde's gait a stomping. It was more like tiptoeing in cowboy boots.

He cooed, "Nice moosey, Gentle moosey."

Amazingly enough, the moose stood her ground, kind of trembling, while Clyde knelt at her side. I think the flip had her discombobulated.

Clyde said, "Cheese is too complicated. I'm leaning toward a line of moose ice cream."

He slid on his latex gloves, placed the bucket in position, leaned his forehead to her flank, took hold of her udder and squeezed.

In the upshot, I flew off Nellie's back end and my saddle flew off the front. The calf ran blindly through Maurey, knocking her into marsh water and voiding the warranty on the I Phone. More than one observer up at the Lodge screamed. Roger cut his losses by cutting his rope.

As far as I know, to this day there's a moose dragging Roger's rope by one leg and my saddle by her throat dangle through the willow flats of Jackson Lake. The rangers refused to tell me what became of her. They weren't as courteous as you expect rangers to be.

We're having a charity fundraiser at the Virginian Bar and Lounge Sunday next, in the evening. All the cheap beer and hot wings you can consume for thirty bucks. Proceeds go to Clyde's rehabilitation, which has been as extensive as you would expect.

WINTER 2010

Way back at the beginning of time when I was but a boy growing up in Duncan, Oklahoma, my parents bought an album by a group called The Chad Mitchell Trio. Music came on vinyl plates back then. The Chad Mithell Trio album was filled with funny songs such as "The John Birch Society" (roots music for Tea Partyers) and "Lizzie Borden" (*Lizzie Borden took an axe and gave her mother 40 whacks*) but the song that sent my sister and I careening off the walls, howling with glee, was "Superskier."

We charged down the hall, screaming, "It's a bird, no, it's a plane. It's *Superskier!*" Mom must have been tempted to flush Chad Mitchell down the toilet.

"Superskier" is the story of a guy with the walk, the talk, and the snappy dress, but in reality he has never strapped on skis in his life. He's the prime stud of après ski. In the song, someone forces him to actually ski and he suffers a crash for the ages.

Flash forward fifty years and I'm talking to my friend Larry Rieser who has been a ski instructor since skis were made from hickory boards. I mentioned my youthful obsession with "Superskier," and Larry said —

"I wrote that song."

Naturally, I said, "No way."

"My wife at the time and I wrote 'Superskier' in Aspen's Limelighter Lounge in 1958."

Being the cynical, tech wienie I am, I hopped on my Droid, shouted "Superskier" into the Voice Search, and there it was — "Superskier" by Rieser/Rieser. Phone internet has taken the drama out of bar bets.

After I went home with new-found respect for Larry, I got to thinking: Does Superskier still haunt downhill powder-land? Do guys (I assumed they were guys. Women would never brag of skill sets they don't possess) still hang around the lounge fireplace, sipping brandy and pontificating on moguls on Thunder when the closest they've ever been to a slope is the wheelchair access at Four Seasons?

The next day, I called Larry and asked him.

"Sure," he said. "Does the Pope wear socks?"

"I'm not certain on that one."

"As long as there are lift lines there will be bullshitters."

"I must meet one."

"You'll have to wear hip waders."

"Are we speaking metaphorically?"

Turns out we were. The next evening, Larry took me to the Hotel Terra in search of the modern Superskier.

We found Slick Rock in the sundeck hot tub, surrounded by the three Statutory Sisters (not their real names.) Slick was deeply, deeply tanned with a silver hoop in his right ear and a BORN TO BOARD tattoo across his shoulders. The sisters giggled appreciatively at every word Slick said.

"It was sick. I was zipper lining the bumps when I launched air over the corn cliff into a daffy gap jump into cookies and bonked a bomb hole big enough for a Port-A-Potty."

"What did he say?" I asked Larry.

Larry said, "He said, 'I have never slid across snow on anything smoother than my butt.'"

Suddenly, one of the sisters (#1) yelped. "Yuck, what's that?" She pointed at something greasy floating in the tub.

Sister #2 said, "It's Slick's tattoo." She turned on Slick. "You swore they weren't henna."

Sister #3 said, "It's not his tattoo. It's his tan coming off."

It was both. As Slick delaminated into the hot tub, the Statutory Sisters splashed to safety and took off, on the hunt for a more authentic hound.

Next step was the Mangy Moose Saloon where Larry introduced me to the female version of Superskier, sometimes referred to as the Snow Bunny. This one was even named Bunny. Angel Bunny, whose real name was Bunny Angel, was bouncing languidly across the dance floor in a Xanax fog. Both hands held shot glasses filled with something the color of jaundiced urine (So Co). Bunny was a vision of winter — fur trimmed jacket (Bogner), ivory cashmere turtleneck (North Face), black leggings (Donatella Versace), mule boots (Uggs) with a wedge heel.

"Surely, this one skis," I said.

"Angel is from Houston," Larry said. "She couldn't buckle on a boot if it came with a free Gucci hand bag."

Angel swung in a circle and sang out the mating cry of the Snow Bunny: "I'm *soooo* drunk!"

The snowboarders circled like jackals closing in on a gazelle with a torn ACL.

Speaking of torn ACLs, a rugged looking, chiseled jaw character with a shaved head and prison biceps sat at the bar, his foot propped on a nearby stool, his leg in a cast.

"That's Gor," Larry said. "He doesn't use a last name."

"Like Cher."

"More like Madonna."

Gor spoke. "I jumped into Corbet's Couloir, stuck the landing, made the first turn and came around a corner into a film crew shooting a dog food commercial right in the middle of the track. It was either wipe out a golden retriever puppy or dry gulch into the rocks."

"What did you do?" asked the youngest Statutory Sister (#3) who had beat us over from Hotel Terra.

"I saved the puppy's life, of course," Gor said. "But the rocks tore my ACL and broke my femur in three places."

Larry said, "He tore his meniscus getting off an escalator at Lego Land six years ago, and he scored a pity date off the girl at the pharmacist's where he went for pain killers. Ever since then, Gor's worn a fake cast and walked on crutches whenever he cruises the scene."

"His leg isn't broken in three places?"

"He's the night stocker at K Mart. I saw him working yesterday and he's normal, for Gor. He wears the cast so he doesn't have to dance. Or ski. He uses it to pick up chicks."

"Does it work?"

Statutory Sister #1 touched Gor on the bicep. She said, "You are so machismo."

He growled, "I only did what had to be done."

"Maybe we should write a new version of 'Superskier'," I said to Larry.

"You do it," he said. "I've had my days of glory."

SUMMER 2011

Here are some tidbits I gave Roger Ramsey and his 10-year-old daughter Scarlet Gilia last summer as we sat in a 90-minute, two-mile bear jam near Sheepeater Cliff in Yellowstone. The first automobile — a Winton, whatever that is — entered Yellowstone Park in 1897, but by 1902 cars were considered so obnoxious they were banned. From then until July 31, 1915, cars were illegal; in 1916, cars and horse-drawn vehicles shared the roads; in 1917, horse-drawn vehicles were outlawed. That's how fast high-tech change comes to America.

The speed limit in 1921 was 15 — 7 on the curves and hills. Drivers were required to honk before going around a curve. Most Yellowstone roads were one-way in the morning and then they reversed and were one-way the other way in the afternoon. Motorcycle rangers could go both ways, but on Dunraven Pass, if they met a car, they had to dismount and lean their Harleys against the inside wall.

Roger said what people always say when I enlighten them with Yellowstone auto trivia.

"So it was quicker to get around Yellowstone in 1921 than it is now."

He said this because we weren't even in sight of the mother

grizzly and four cubs that we knew were gamboling in a meadow two miles ahead. We knew on account of that mama and cubs had been creating the greatest bear jam in park history for over a week and we'd decided to drive to Mammoth for an ice cream cone anyway. You almost have to be from Wyoming to understand why driving four hours for an ice cream cone isn't weird.

Scarlet Gilia said, "My summer camp teacher says that not all four of those cubs belong to the mother by birth. She's babysitting one or two."

"Grizzly bears don't babysit," I said.

"Are you saying Miss Crabapple is a liar?"

"The girl has got a point," Roger said. "Grizzly bears don't have four cubs anymore than they babysit. Something unlikely is going on."

"I daresay the mother was assigned the spare cub by the Wildlife Traffic Combine."

We moved two car lengths forward but came up short behind a Winnebago parked more or less on the shoulder, totally abandoned as the owner and his extended family marched off up the highway, camera-laden, in search of grizzly bears.

"This is your fault," Roger said.

He blamed me because I went to a public hearing and spoke against the six-lane with double shoulders and entrance ramps highway that Roger and others of his ilk tried to ram down the park's metaphorical throat.

Locals are fairly evenly divided between those who want Yellowstone's roads better and those who want Yellowstone's roads worse. No one likes them the way they are.

I am in the worse contingent. It's a national park, for God's sake. What's the hurry? It's a known fact that 92% of all Yellowstone visitors never go more than fifteen yards from pavement.

"Who established this known fact?" Roger asked.

"Everyone knows it's a known fact. We should join the WTC and make Yellowstone's roads as slow as can be."

"Okay, Uncle Tim," Scarlet Gilia said. "I'll bite. Tell us your crazy WTC theory." I like Scarlet Gilia.

"My dear mother was the first to tell me about Wildlife Traffic Combine," I said. "Back in the 60s when we counted 23 bears between the South Entrance and Old Faithful."

"Whatever happened to all those bears?" Scarlet Gilia asked.

Roger and I exchanged a grown-up look. According to the Park Service, there was a bad winter and hundreds of black bears died because they'd been fed Cheetos. According to everyone else in northwest Wyoming, the rangers gunned down the beggars.

I decided against scarring the girl for life. Like all adults faced with a tough question, I ignored her.

"My mom told me the bears met in the spring, in Fountain Flats, to divide up the roads and campgrounds. The old, respected bears were given campgrounds where bear-proof trash cans were but a dream and the tourists loved to snap Kodaks of bears eating out their kids' hands."

"Miss Crabapple says hand-feeding bears is foolish."

"How many times have I told you not to listen to Miss Crabapple," Roger said.

I plowed on. "The powerful bears got Roosevelt Lodge to Cooke City and along the Gibbon River while the red-headed step-children bears were assigned to Lewis Canyon. Mom hated Lewis Canyon. There weren't guard rails back then."

In a daring, reckless maneuver, Roger zipped around the Winnebago and almost hit a woman wearing an outfit made entirely out of pinking sheared beer cans.

"After the bear kill-off, the WTC hibernated for a few years until there was so much roadkill the summer of the Yellowstone fires that the animals brought it back."

"Is this one of Uncle Tim's tall tales?" Scarlet Gilia asked.

"Mom says he wouldn't know the truth if came out of a raven's rear end and landed on his head."

"Funny you should mention ravens," I said. "They're the ones who organize the spring conference. All the park wildlife comes together on a Sunday afternoon to choose what species get what stretches of road to cause the maximum in traffic disruption.

"This year the conference was held at Heart Lake. As luck would have it, I was the only human invited."

"You're always the only human invited to magic meetings," Scarlet Gilia said. "Why is that?"

"The ravens flipped a coin. The wolves got Dunraven and Lamar Valley. Black bears took the roads around Old Faithful. Grizzlies from Madison to Mammoth."

"Thus they are right here, where we are," Roger said.

"Thus proving I'm not making this up," I said. "Only grizzlies with cubs can back traffic up over a mile."

"Where are the moose, Uncle Tim?" Scarlet Gilia asked.

"West Thumb, mostly. And around Lake Hotel. A few were assigned to Firehole Canyon. The sandhill cranes filed a protest over Craig Pass. Said they'd been grandfathered up there since Chief Joseph granted them an exclusive to Shoshone Lake for giving him the 'I will fight no more forever' line. It brought the process to chaos until the young wolves ate the sandhills."

"What about bison?"

I want to throw up when I hear kids call buffalo bison. What's education come to these days? "Buffalo aren't in the WTC. They got caught horning in on an elk jam a couple years ago and were banished to the backcountry. So they quit the combine and now they go anywhere they want. You can't stop a buffalo who wants his picture taken."

"But, Uncle Tim," Scarlet Gilia said. "That doesn't make sense."

"What part of it doesn't make sense?" I asked.

"Ravens can't flip coins."

Roger said, "The girl has got a point there," just as a Harley biker strayed over from Sturgis drove into our back end.

WINTER 2011

Heather Heidi Walsowski-Smith's daughter, Columbine, is researching a school project on pioneer migration into Jackson Hole. Her task is to interview old-timers who came here in the 1970s and 80s, to see how they arrived and why they stayed. She caught up with me with my hose down a mole hole, trying to flush the buggers from my lawn.

"Are you an old-timer?" Columbine asked.

A plaintive squeak came from nearby, but no rodent bodies floated to the surface. "I'm more a middle aged-timer," I said. "You have to go back two generations of home birth to qualify as a true old-timer."

"Why did you move to Jackson?"

"It was semi-unplanned."

"All my interviewees say that. I haven't met a single person who chose to spend their lives in the valley. They come temporary, but stay permanent."

"You want my story or not?"

Columbine pulled out her phone and opened a tape recorder app. Columbine's life is composed of apps. A mole broke free over on the driveway side of the yard. It scampered for the neighbor's lawn and I wished it well. I think that's where they migrated from in the first place. He puts out poison and they head for me.

"I was on vacation with my family. 1968."

"The Dark Ages," Columbine said. "Did you have cars back then?"

"We had cars without air conditioning, so family vacations were another word for hell. Shut up and listen to my story." Another mole made a break and I turned off the hose. "We ate lunch at Signal Mountain Lodge and the waitress offered me a dishwashing job. Both dishwashers had quit in a huff and she was desperate. I said, 'Let me ask my parents,' and they said, 'See you in September.' I've been here ever since."

"Your mom and dad ditched you in the middle of a vacation?"

"They couldn't get out of the parking lot fast enough. Dad left a $20 tip." I gave up on the moles. Let them have the lawn. It never did much for me, and I didn't become a nature lover to grow up and drown rats.

"That is so sad," Columbine said. "I always wondered what it was in your past that warped you so badly."

I decided not to ask the obvious follow-up question to that one. Instead, I went with, "What other stories have you heard?"

Columbine pulled out a notebook — the paper kind — and flipped back through the pages. "Mom graduated from Colorado State and decided to ski one winter before settling down into a career in marketing analysis."

"And she never left."

"Dad was driving from the East Coast to law school in San Francisco. He detoured through Yellowstone. Threw a rod on Teton Pass."

"And never left."

"Kasey Cutestuff spent two weeks at a dude ranch in the Gros Ventres. Fell in love with a cowboy."

"And never left."

"But the cowboy did. He sells RVs in Oxnard, California,

now. George Dandy was best man at his college roommate's wedding out at Crescent H. The bridesmaid got pregnant."

"And George never left."

"Not a one of them came here with a plan. Natalie Foxcroft and Holly Hamm were cabin maids at Old Faithful. Midway through the northern lights they discovered they didn't like boys. They fell in love, moved into a Kelly yurt, and opened a riding stable."

"They're still out there. They run a secret bull castration ceremony of empowerment."

"Roger Ramsey got drunk in the Mangy Moose, spent thirty days in the Teton County jail, and by the time they cut him loose he loved the valley so much he opened a frozen yogurt stand."

I wound up the hose. God knows I've tried lawn care. It just doesn't work for me. My yard will always be wilderness. No doubt I'll soon have a pack of wolves. "Lots of stories start with a seasonal job followed by true love that moves into choosing a day care center."

Columbine peered down at her notes. "The ones who came single and fell in love tend to last. Kids who move here as couples rarely stick together."

"They can't deal with the stigma of couplehood in a valley full of singles. Lots of women with boyfriends deny it right up to marriage."

Columbine found the example she'd been looking for. "Clay Nation was camping with his fiancée Pepper in Curtis Canyon. He woke up to a note that read, GONE SHOPPING. Pepper took the Dodge Colt, their dog, and both credit cards. He was stuck in the woods with nothing but a tent and a double-wide sleeping bag. After four days of waiting, he hitched into town and got a job at the first restaurant he came to."

"That would be the Lame Duck."

"Clay waited for 25 years. At the interview, he got all wimpy-eyed telling me about that dog." She flipped forward to the end of the notebook. "The tragic stories are the kids who are born here and try to leave but fail."

"All high school kids blame misery on their home towns. It's the American way."

"Jennilyn Molesworth took off graduation night, swearing she would never return. First, she hit Portland, then Seattle."

"Portland and Seattle are halfway houses for Jackson teenagers. It's a rite of passage thing."

"Jennilyn's mother offered her a plane ticket home for Christmas. Freaked Jennilyn out so bad she ran to Fairbanks, Alaska. When her mom sent a Valentine's card, Jennilyn left for Wake Island. Later, she surfaced at a jungle outpost in New Guinea, but her grandfather died and her mom shamed her on Facebook into flying home for the funeral."

"I can see how this ends."

"At the cemetery, Jennilyn tripped over the backpack she had ready for her escape. She fell in the hole and broke her ankle. It's been ten years now and she's still in her parents' spare room."

"Doesn't take ten years for an ankle to heal."

"Her mom says if Jennilyn doesn't do what her mom wants, it will kill her dad."

"How often have I heard that one."

Columbine gathered up her phone and notebook, ready to move on to her next old-timer. "You won't see me stuck in my parents' town. Come summer, I'm down the road."

"All roads lead back home."

"Not mine."

"Look at it this way. The Jackson metaphor is a cosmic toilet and when God flushes all our children are sucked home through the pipe. That's why they call us a Hole."

"Yuck, Tim. You are disgusting."

"I'll take that in a good way."

Author's note: All case histories in this story are true. The names have been changed because I don't write nonfiction.

SUMMER 2012

Writers and sociologists love to divide humanity into mutually exclusive groups. For example, those who look forward to slurping raw oysters and those who would rather snort barbwire. Those who like playing in snow, and those whose faith system includes hibernation. Those who think "American Idol" is choice, quality entertainment and the rest of the civilized world

In Jackson Hole, I have observed a sharp division between locals who correct tourists spreading misinformation and locals who, when confronted by an out-of-towner, lie.

I mentioned this to my friend Heather Heidi Walsowski-Smith at our weekly coffee break at Pearl Street Bagels. Heather Heidi comes to the coffee shop directly from a Zumba class at the Center for the Arts, so she feels compelled to replace lost calories. She calls it a Yin Yang balance thing. Sweat must be countered with sugar, fat, and caffeine. She ordered a caramel triple shot latte with whipped cream and a poppy seed bagel swathed in mixed berry cream cheese.

I talked while she uploaded. "My mother couldn't stand it when tourists screwed up their nature lore. The first time I saw her jump into a conversation, I was ten years old and embarrassed by everything odd my parents did or said. We were at Old Faithful, standing next to a gentleman in a sweater vest from London or Australia or someplace where they spell *parlour* with a _u_, and this guy was telling his family — in English — that those furry rodents popping out from under the boardwalk were beavers.

"Mom jumped in. 'They're marmots.'

"The Commonwealth man said, 'Pardon?'

"Mom said, "Some people call them rock chucks, but in Wyoming we say marmot.' Mom wasn't even from Wyoming. She was raised in Oklahoma where it's perfectly normal to insert yourself into overheard conversations."

Heather Heidi spoke through purple glop. "I doubt if that's kosher in London."

"The prig man didn't thank Mom for making him look stupid in front of his family. Mom didn't care. She'd hear *Elf Refuge* or some yahoo planning to ride the Gros Ventre Slide and she'd wade in with updated truth. She wouldn't even drop it when a stranger mispronounced *Gros Ventre*."

"My husband goes spastic when people say *TEE-tons* instead of tea-TAHNS. You'd think they insulted Poland." She chugged 700 milligrams of caffeine in a single gulp. "And don't even get me started on *Dubois*. I'd rather hear fingernails on a chalkboard than some coastal snob acting like *Dubois* is a French word."

I sipped green tea. I've been chasing my coffee with green tea ever since I heard an expert on the Ellen DeGeneris Show who said if I drink green tea I'll live forever.

"Involvement with strangers is a Southern habit," I said. "Not Western. You sit next to a weeping woman on an airplane, a Southerner will offer her a Kleenex and call her *Honey*. A Wyoming native, on the other hand, won't say a word. He'll figure if the woman wants a Kleenex, she'll ask for it, and if she does ask for a Kleenex this theoretical Wyoming native will turn the airplane inside out to get her one."

"What about New Yorkers?"

"A New Yorker will sneak into First Class."

I drank tea while H.H. went to the counter to put a quarter in the chocolate covered coffee beans machine. She came back, popping a handful into her mouth. Frankly, I'm not certain why she bothers with Zumba.

"My dad was the opposite of your mom," Heather Heidi said. 'If a tourist called a marmot a weasel he'd tell them, no, those are baby bears. Used to drive me insane when I was a teenager."

"We had a naturalist at Jenny Lake who would tell tourists moose are mature elk, and an antelope can be trained to play the xylophone. He said that's what the song means by *Deer and the antelope play.* Tourist saw the green uniform and the Rings of Saturn ranger hat and they believed him. A naturalist wouldn't lie.

"He's the one showed me Jackson Hole in an outhouse before he knew I lived here. He offered to take my photograph next to it."

"I doubt if the Park Service would allow rangers to lie today," Heather Heidi said. "Modern times have gone anal."

"Locals the world over lie to outsiders," I said. "It makes them feel superior to prove the rubes don't know basic stuff."

"My grandfather bought the Brooklyn Bridge from a cab driver. It's the family shame."

"That's my point. If the Brooklyn cab driver had been here your grandfather would have told him drinking horse urine will protect you from rattlesnakes. Everyone is clueless somewhere."

"My wife's from Hawaii. Her friends would tell mainland cool kids that if you lick a gecko you'll go on a psychedelic trip and meet Pele. Then they'd sit back and laugh at the Ivy Leaguers licking lizards."

"Heck," Heather Heidi said. "If Tralfamdorians came to Earth we'd laugh at them for taking dolphins as the intelligent species and talking to them instead of us."

"You remember that story I wrote about Day Care Air," I

said. "The airline for children of divorced parents with split custody. No seats. Licensed pre-school teachers for flight attendants."

"It went viral," Heather Heidi said. "You gave my phone number as the reservation clerk and I had to handle the onslaught of calls."

"The thing is, I didn't dream anyone would buy it. I make up these stories about snow snakes or nuns living in secret caves on Mount Moran and then perfectly nice people believe me and if I tell them it's a joke they get huffy so I keep my mouth shut but I feel like a boy squishing June bugs."

"Nuns in Mount Moran?"

"That one may be true. I'm not sure. The Arapaho legend has it that if Delta ever brings a flight in on time and with every passenger's luggage, nine nuns will dance down the mountain singing the Shondell's version of 'Crimson and Clover' while doing cartwheels through the buttercups."

Heather Heidi gave me one of her special looks of skepticism. "And you think this might be true, but you're not sure?"

"It's never been tested," I said. "Delta has never held up its end of he legend."

WINTER 2012

The first decent blizzard of winter Clyde Walsowski-Smith and I drove my new Honda Accord over Teton Pass on our way to Idaho Falls for Clyde's laughter therapy. His wife, Heather Heidi, read where laughing relieves stress so she signed Clyde up for this class where a famous therapist teaches Idahoans how to giggle. According the therapist, Idahoans don't laugh properly. Instead of sounding like a mountain stream bubbling over moss-covered rocks, Idahoans laugh like a potato would, if a potato laughed. More of a guttural mumble — *Huh, huh.*

Anyway, driving Teton Pass in a blizzard on your way to a stress reduction session is one of those examples of irony. White outs came and went and we had to guess which side of the snow poles was paved. Naturally, as happens when plowing through a snowstorm, conversation turned to virgin winter drivers. Clyde's new neighbors from Odessa, Texas, put chains on their BMW SUV snow tires in mid-September and never took them off come wet roads or dry till a chain broke, wrapped around the drive shaft, and sent them sailing through a GIVE A MOOSE A BRAKE sign.

"Their house is up for sale," Clyde said.

"My wife read on the internet that you should drive in first gear whenever snow is falling. She said it's the only way to avoid out-of-control hysteria."

"There should be a law against wives trolling the Internet," Clyde said. "Heather Heidi Googled a story that said coffee causes heart attacks. I countered with ten said it prevents them, but she claims her one trumps my ten and I'm stuck on Oolong."

I said, "The internet is like the Bible. You look around a while you can always find what you want to hear. And then you can ignore all the other stuff."

At this point a woman driving a brand new Lincoln Town Car with South Carolina plates blew past us going about 60. Backwards. I got a quick glance at her — 30-something, copper-colored hair, squash blossom necklace over a sub-zero down parka — with her arm across the passenger seat and her head twisted to see the road behind. She did a competent job, considering she was flying up the hill in reverse.

Clyde and I watched the headlights come back into our lane as she receded up the highway in the blowing snow. As men will when they share an experience that makes no sense, neither one of us acknowledged what had just happened.

Clyde said, "Speaking of hearing what you want in the Bible, did you read about that cracker who insists his employees abide by a *Biblical definition of marriage?*"

"God, I hope you aren't turning political. Politics have become a cyst on a boil on the buttocks of America."

"I'm talking Biblical definitions of marriage. I checked it out –"

"On the internet."

"And the proto-typical Biblical marriage is an old guy with four wives and a bunch of slave concubines. I can't find a straight one man-one woman marriage in the Old Testament."

"The guy who said *Biblical family* meant he doesn't want gay partners on his group insurance. He was falling back on that verse in Leviticus about a man sleeping with a man is an abomination, but a woman with a woman isn't."

Clyde was so worked up he slapped the glove compartment. "Have you read Leviticus? Shaving or cutting your hair is an abomination. Eating clams and lobsters in an abomination. A woman can't leave her house for seven days after her period. A child who curses his parents much be immediately killed."

"My daughter should use that verse for a screen saver."

"It even says you'll go to hell for playing football."

"English or American?"

"Any person who touches the skin of a pig must immediately kill a pigeon over clean water in a clay pot, or be forever damned."

"I don't think they make footballs out of pig skin anymore."

"Okay, only old football players are forever damned."

I considered the implications in light of an after school snack my mom used to push on me in grade school. "So what you are saying is the religious right quotes Leviticus when it says what they want to hear, and they ignore it when they eat clam chowder."

"Don't even get me started on Deuteronomy."

We came around that big sweeping curve before Glory Bowl and there was the Lincoln Town car axle deep in the ditch. As we pulled over to help, I couldn't help but notice the woman had the accelerator floored so the engine was winding up like a Lear jet at take off and the tires spinning like grandmothers in their graves.

Clyde and I got out, walked over, and made roll-down-your-window signals. When she did, Clyde said, "Take your foot off the gas, ma'am."

"I can't. I'm melting snow."

"You're making enough ice for a hockey rink. Ease up."

She eased up. "Arnold says if you spin the tires fast enough the heat will melt you out of any snow drift."

"And Arnold is?"

"My husband. He knows every trick to driving in winter. He once lived in Oklahoma."

I knelt to check out the tires. Clyde said, "Is Arnold the one told you going in reverse is the same as front-wheel drive?"

"No, duh. A rear-wheel drive car becomes a front-wheel car when you drive it backwards. Everyone knows that."

"Did Arnold have you cram paper clips into your tire tread grooves?" I asked.

"They provide traction."

Clyde knelt beside me to admire the hundreds of paper clips pushed into the tread grooves. "Why didn't I think of that?" Clyde said.

"Because it doesn't work."

Clyde stood and leaned against the Town Car roofline. "Your husband is out to kill you, ma'am. Give me the keys."

"Are you stealing my car?"

I said, "Why should we steal a stuck car when we have a perfectly good Honda.

Clyde said, "Jesus said you should never brag about a Honda.'

"I've got to hear this."

"John 12:49 — *For I did not speak of my own Accord.*" He leaned down to look in at the woman. "We're opening the trunk so we can jack up the car and save you from death."

The woman handed Clyde the keys. "Arnold says most car jackings are initiated by Good Samaritans with an agenda."

"Arnold is an idiot," Clyde said as he popped the trunk.

And there he was. Arnold, in the flesh. I'd have picked him out in a crowd of thousands. Pastel dress shirt, skinny tie, boxy glasses hanging off a ribbon around his neck. That haircut you find on gays, missionaries, and Ralph Nader.

I said, "I'm on pins and needles to hear why you're in the trunk. Is your reason Biblical?"

"It's Yahoo News," Arnold said. "The safest place to store valuables in the trunk."

"But you're not valuable," I said.

"First Samuel, 10:22," Clyde said. *"Behold he has hid himself among the baggage."*

I stared at Clyde in wonder. "You're not a Thumper. Since when did you learn all these creepy quotes?"

"Laugh therapy," Clyde said. "The famous therapist uses Bible verses for punch lines."

All I could think of to say was this: "Oh."

SUMMER 2013

The talk of the town this past winter was our very own bank robbery. New Year's Eve, an Australian self-help author named Cory Donaldson borrowed his friend's Toyota Tundra and drove up from Utah to rob the U.S. Bank. We don't know why he didn't hit a bank closer to home, or why he borrowed a truck if he planned to park in front of security cameras. All we know is Cory got $140,000 and change and drove away into the sunset.

He was caught twenty-two days later, in a taxicab, with only $20,000 left of the money. Cory claims he gave the rest to the homeless. The only person in Teton County who believes that story is an old woman up Game Creek with a neck wider around than her head and a firm belief in intelligent design. For one thing, Cory said he gave $15,000 to the Reno Salvation Army, but no one at the Reno Salvation Army recalls the gift. If he's falling back on the Robin Hood defense, Cory should have asked for receipts.

The rampant rumor around town is that Cory hid the money. The thought process — at least in the Jackson Hole High lunchroom — is he ditched at least $100,000 before he left town, knowing the borrowed truck would sooner or later lead to grief. His plan is to make bail, come pick up his money, and then flee back to Australia where he has a large family who look at him as a scamp.

Over Spring Break, Heather Heidi and Clyde Walsowski-Smith's daughter, Columbine, organized a treasure hunt. Five of us — Clyde, H-H, Columbine, me, and Maurey Pierce — met at Pearl Street Bagels.

"It was winter when he took the money," Clyde said. "That cuts down considerably on hidey holes."

"He must have stashed it in a culvert," Heather Heidi said.

Columbine was drinking a double latte, which I wouldn't have allowed had she been my daughter. She said, "What's a culvert."

Kids these days. I tried to explain the theory of highway drainage. She never did get it till Maurey showed her a photo on Instagram.

"Oh," Columbine said. "A pipe."

"A big pipe."

"How much space would $100,000 in cash take up?" Heather Heidi asked.

We all conjectured based on the two tens and a Bagel Buck I had in my billfold, but it was beyond reasonable expectations without an idea of the original denominations.

Maurey said, "Unless they were thousand dollar bills, they wouldn't fit in a purse."

"Cory didn't look like a guy with a purse," Clyde said. "My guess is duffel. Or laundry bag."

"Bird houses," Heather Heidi said. "He broke up the money and stuck it in birdhouses, figuring he'd be back before the birds. There's hundreds of bird houses between here and Utah."

"How about an abandoned mail box," I said. "The rural delivery kind with the little red flag that flips up."

"Or an osprey nest," Maurey said. "Nobody would see it in an osprey next."

Clyde said, "A hollow tree."

Bottom line is the five of us split up to search all the likely spots in Teton County. I assigned myself abandoned mailboxes, only I didn't find any, so I came back empty handed.

Two hours later the others reconvened at the bagel shop. They had found sixty-two cents in dull change, three sandwich baggies of marijuana, a tiny cutter race trophy, a plastic cup advertising Jake's Cosmetic Surgery, a quart jar of elk turds, a rusted cell phone, and a Geo Cache logbook. Columbine also found a dead cat but she didn't bring it inside the bagel shop. No hundred thousand dollars.

"I think he mailed it to himself in Ecuador," Heather Heidi said. "That's what the bank robbers did on Hawaii Five O."

I looked up Cory's website — AnalyzeMyWife.com — on my smartphone. Analyzing failed relationships is what Corey did for a living before he turned to robbing banks. He also published two self-help books, *Don't You Dare Get Married Until You Read This!* and *Don't You Dare Have Kids Until You Read This!* The website was down but the Amazon bio did mention he was a divorced guy with no kids.

"You think there's a lot of cash flow in self-help?" I asked.

"Must be," Maurey said. "Hundreds of them come out every year. They have their own section at the bookstore."

"I always had the urge to write a self-help book about relationships," Heather Heidi said.

Her husband *guffawed.* That the only word for it. *Guffaw.* "What would you know about relationships?"

"I've been married to you thirty years. That either makes me a saint or a superhero."

This sparked my curiosity. "So what would you say in a self-help book? I need all the wisdom I can get."

Heather Heidi drummed her fingers on the table. "Okay, here's the most important lesson I've learned from life.

"Don't stay in a motel with a sign our front that says CLEAN RESTROOMS.

Maurey said, "Do not pick up hitchhikers wearing camouflage."

Columbine said, "Never buy macaroni and cheese cheaper than Kraft."

The wisdom came quicker now with each of us chiming in. "Don't make ice cream out of yellow snow."

"Don't buy electronics from a man without teeth."

"Don't put your real birthday on Facebook."

"Don't mix toothpaste with thirty-weight oil."

"Don't use *transition* as a verb. People will know you're pompous." That one was from me.

"Don't hire a babysitter who has LOVE and HATE tattooed on her knuckles."

"When casting a fly rod upwind, use a barbless hook."

"Never eat blue food."

"People who live in tin houses shouldn't throw can openers."

"Don't send money to a woman in Chad who says she'll give you thirty million dollars if you'll only help her get it out of the country."

"Don't forward jokes or pictures of cute cats."

"Don't pee in the light socket," Columbine said.

"What?"

"You told me that over and over when I was a kid."

"That's all valid information." I poured honey into my latte, which is not something the others did. "But we'll never sell books unless you write about love. Nobody really cares about macaroni and cheese.

"I do."

"Don't you have any wise words for the dating set?"

Clyde went first. "Powder and paint makes 'em what they ain't. Padding and stuffing, don't add nothing."

Heather Heidi gave Clyde a look that women can pull off and men can't. "Stay away from men who curse in the backcountry. If they can't find peace in the woods, they can't find peace."

Clyde: "Beware of women in wigs."

Heather Heidi, "If he says, 'I have a bad history with credit cards,' pass him by."

Clyde: "Stay clear of women who don't eat."

I jumped in. "Don't go out with anyone who uses five or more adjectives to order coffee."

Heather Heidi: "If a man looks too good to be true, he is."

Maurey: "Never marry a man who has more prescriptions than you."

Heather Heidi: "Separated is not the same as divorced."

Columbine: "Don't sleep with your roommate."

"How do you know that?" Clyde asked.

"You don't want to know."

I said, "You lose them the way you get them, so if he cheats on someone to be with you he'll feel free to cheat on you."

Maurey: "Nobody changes."

Heather Heidi: "The one thing worse than losing your first true love is not losing your first true love."

Columbine said, "That's sad."

"But true."

"Cory should write another book from prison," I said. "He could call it *Don't You Dare Borrow a Truck to Rob a Bank Then Park It in Front of a Surveillance Camera Until You've Read This!*"

Clyde said, "Kind of a long title, don't you think?"

"Yeah, well, he's going to be serving a long sentence."

WINTER 2013

George and Jazmyne Finch recently committed the faux pas that leads so many Jackson Hole newcomers to ruin. After five years of living here, they married and bought a house. Getting married and buying a house aren't the faux pas I'm talking about. You can harbor your own cynical to romantic notions of a marriage lasting in paradise.

George and Jazmyne's fatal error was they bought a house with more bedrooms than they needed. The cute couple went so far as to buy a three-bedroom home — two more than they would occupy for sleeping and watching late-night TV.

George had a vague plan for a home office — he's a drywall contractor, and Jazmyne, an elementary school teacher, had an even vaguer plan for babies in the distant future. They still could have minimized the damage by collecting a mountain of sports junk and filling the rooms to the point of no safe entry. Instead, Jazmyne said, "Our loved ones can visit. We'll have a place for them to stay."

I said, "Famous last words."

Any long-term local could have told them Jackson Hole abhors a vacuum. If you have space, they will come.

George said, "We love guests."

I said, "Right."

First, Jazmyne's cousins Dothan and Opp showed up for hunting season. The cousins installed an arsenal and a pony keg in the spare bedroom. Dothan said, "We'll be in the field all day. You won't even know we're here."

The word *field* should have set off bells. Dothan and Opp were from south Texas where hunting is done in a field. Their version of fair chase is to sit in a lawn chair in the bed of a pickup truck, sipping Jim Beam and blasting feral pigs. When George told them you can't kill Wyoming animals from a pickup truck they got so disgusted at the federal government's interference with their God-given rights they decided to drink the keg and watch ESPN till their vacation was over.

The day Dothan and Opp finally cleared out, George's roommate from prep school — Chet — showed up with his lovely wife and two precocious toddlers. George and Chet greeted each other with a secret handshake and called each other preppie names — *Camel* for George, *Stone Fly* for Chet. Camel referred to an old joke about one hump or two that Jazmyne had no desire to hear.

Chet's wife — LouLou — said Jazmyne wasn't doing anything anyway so would she babysit the kids while she and Chet went on a tour of historical bars of Jackson Hole? Chet brought up a sacred oath to shame George into going with them.

After a week of this, Jazmyne rebelled against babysitting the brats and Stone Fly and LouLou left in a huff. The friendship of a lifetime was destroyed.

The very airplane that swept Chet away brought in Annabel and Murray Oaks, golfing buddies of Jazmyne's Aunt Holly, the aunt Jazmyne hadn't seen since middle school graduation.

"Holly made us promise we'd look you up. She said she'd never forgive us if we came all this way and didn't say *howdy*. Do you know a hotel that takes smokers? We can only afford thirty dollars a night."

So Annabel and Murray moved in with their skis, a commercial grade espresso machine, and veritable array of IPods, Pads, and Phones, not to mention a machine that made city noises so they could sleep at night. Not that Murray slept. He had perfected a ratio of vodka to Red Bull that enabled him to stay awake and drunk for days on end. The Oaks skied all day while George and Jazmyne worked their jobs, then they insisted on taking the Finches out every night — Dutch treat. This might never have ended had Annabel not blown an ACL. Murray said, "Thanks a bunch," and left her. After four days of waiting on Annabel like a bumptious servant, George bought her a first-class plane ticket — can't expect a woman with a bad knee to sit in coach — home.

Next came Jazmyne's mother. Mildred has high blood pressure, osteoarthritis, stage four anxiety, and a spastic colon. She can't be left alone. George had to take off work to care for her. Mildred watches nothing but reality TV and she can't hear, so our cute couple was blasted out of the house by *Say Yes to the Dress* and *Duck Dynasty*.

A few days after Mildred's arrival, Cassie Strong telephoned. Since Cassie lives in Teton Village, Jazmyne picked up the phone. She was over out-of-town caller I.D.s, but she felt safe with local numbers.

Fat chance. Cassie said, "I'm in charge of housing for the Up With People crew coming to town and since you have so much room, I put you down for three girls. They'll be no trouble. All you have to do is feed them and drive them to their appointments.

Yeah, well, feed them. One girl had a wheat allergy, another was lactose intolerant, and the third was strict vegan — she couldn't eat plants cooked in a pan that had ever touched meat. Their hair paraphernalia blew a fuse before each performance.

The one good thing to come from housing three Up With People singers for a week was Jazmyne got over her desire for babies. She said, "If wholesome girls are this much work, I'm not about to risk raising a normal kid."

The other good thing is her mother flew back to her brother's house in Hawaii.

The straw that broke Camel's back, so to speak, landed when the wife of Bibs Colander — a counselor at Jazmyne's school — kicked Bibs out of the house. George said, "Absolutely not," but after two nights of Bibs' sleeping in his car at twenty-five below zero, George caved.

He said, "Three days and he's out of here. No more."

More famous last words. Bibs' moving in would not have put the Finch house on the real estate market, in and of itself, but Bibs brought four cats and a box turtle.

"He also has a snake," Jazmyne said. "Big honker, like a fire hose. I think the snake is what motivated his wife to boot him."

"A python, I suppose," George said.

She nodded. "Named Monty."

"Of course, nobody names pythons anything else."

It goes without saying that the snake escaped, ate one of the cats, slithered into the crawl space, and died.

Bottom line: George hopped on the internet and found the American town least likely to be visited by tourists. You know what I'm talking about — Zanesville, Ohio. The Finches sold their Jackson home almost immediately to a young couple from Tennessee who wanted room for loved ones to visit, and they bought a two-story, five-bedroom home in Zanesville with money left over for a twelve-jet hot tub and a gazebo.

I got an email from Jazmyne last week. "We have lived in Zanesville a year now and have not had a single houseguest. This is the true paradise."

SUMMER 2014

Last August as I relaxed on my favorite rock along the shores of Jenny Lake, basking in the sunlight, admiring the shape of a cloud wisping off Teewinot, absorbing the song of birds, a couple in their middle ages approached. They wore clunky hiking boots and what, in my youth, were called Bermuda shorts. Maybe they still are called Bermuda shorts for all I know. The shorts were matching plaids and they both had on basketball warm-up jackets with an Oklahoma City Thunder logo across the chest.

The woman carried a leather-bound notebook. She looked down at the notebook and said, "What is this?"

The man, who had a small wiry dog in a shoulder sling, approached me. "What is this?"

I said, "Jenny Lake."

He turned back to the woman. "Jenny Lake."

The woman plucked one of those pencil stubs they give out at golf courses from behind her ear and checked off a column in the book. She said, "Next, Chapel of Transfiguration," and they both turned and walked away. Neither one so much as glanced at the lake, the mountains, the cloud, or the birds. Jenny Lake — CHECK — and away they went.

I've lived in Jackson Hole long enough to be familiar with checklist tourists, and, while they continue to amaze me no end, I confess to a certain jadedness. If travelers would rather check off an experience than experience the experience, that's their lookout. No skin off my rear. They're not so much worse than those who photograph yet never see. Or Facebook — *I'm at Jenny Lake* — without feeling the sun on their skin.

A couple days later I ran into our plaid Bermuda shorts couple again, this time at Old Faithful. I go to Old Faithful to watch people. Out of their natural habitat, strangers in a strange land, the crowd encircling Old Faithful has been stripped of their veneer. They are delaminated to the core. I'm planning to self-publish a book of ridiculous quotes I have heard on the Old Faithful plastic particleboard boardwalk.

"The Bellagio is bigger."

"An earthquake dried up the original but the Park had too much invested in development so they pipe it in."

"Run up and stick your thumb in the hole. I'll take your picture."

"They turn it off in the winter."

"I'd rather shop."

Anyway, the man in the Bermuda shorts walked to a sign that read OLD FAITHFUL. He turned to his wife and said, "Old Faithful."

CHECK!

I followed them out to the parking lot where they went to a Chevy Sliverado pulling a fifth wheel trailer. The woman opened the trailer door and the dog flew into her arms.

She kissed the dog a wet one right on its lips. "Fluff Puff, my little girl! Did you miss us?"

I said, "Excuse me."

They both turned to me as if being accosted by random strangers is normal, which proves they were from Oklahoma.

"I couldn't help but notice you checked Old Faithful off

your list, but you didn't look at it. You did the same at Jenny Lake two days ago."

The old man said, "Jenny Lake?"

The woman pressed an index finger to her dimpled chin, thinking. "Jenny Lake. Three minutes."

"You spent all of three minutes on the most beautiful lake in the world?"

"Milton's boots came undone. We're generally quicker with lakes."

Milton's face crumpled like wadding up a sheet of yellow legal pad paper. "Fluff Puff took too long on her business. Wasn't my fault we got behind schedule."

I studied Fluff Puff. She was a Pomeranian mix without teeth. She bared her black gums at me and emitted one of those squeaks you hear from dogs who have had their voice boxes surgically removed. Someone here was big on control.

"I would think being on schedule and being on vacation are mutually exclusive."

"Fat lot you know." The woman fished in her huge vinyl purse and for one frightening moment I thought she might pull out photos of loved ones. I would be expected to comment. I hate that. Only thing worse is when your brother-in-law insists on showing you his apps.

Instead, she brought out the leather-bound notebook.

Milton said, "Marlene, you don't have to show that to ever stranger comes along."

Marlene said, "The boy is interested."

I said, "I'm fascinated."

"This here is our bucket list. We each made one on the thirty-fifth anniversary of our wedding, when the alternative was divorce by boredom."

Milton scratched an ear that glowed pink from eczema. "Our Christian therapist said if we didn't do something away from the TV we would wind up shooting each other with our constitutionally protected handguns."

"So you made bucket lists." Personally, I've never approved of the bucket list phenomenon. It's a listing of experiences you want before you kick the bucket. *Kick the bucket* used to mean suicide — you stand on a bucket, put a noose around your neck, secure the far end of the rope, then kick the bucket — but now it means die by any means. Bucket lists focus your life on death. I'd rather do stuff for fun.

"Marlene's list had 126 stops. Mine had 127."

"Milton wanted the Egyptian pyramids. I'd rather get my hair done."

I looked over the list. Eiffel Tower. Graceland. World's largest barbed wire ball in Shelby, South Dakota. More than half the items had pencil checks on their left.

"I'm betting you went all the way to the Eiffel Tower and didn't look at it."

"Wasn't time. We had to bag the Mona Lisa and Van Gogh's ear before five o'clock, French Time Zone."

"I didn't know Van Gogh's ear is a destination."

"We saw the sign for it. We were in the presence and that's good enough for the bucket list. I didn't see any point in looking at a detached ear."

"They wouldn't let Fluff Puff in France so we did the whole country in one day," Marlene said.

Milton sniffed. "France is overrated. We shouldn't have put the nation on our list in the first place."

I handed the notebook back to Marlene. "What did you think of Wyoming?"

"It's dry," Milton said.

Marlene nodded. "Too dry. Makes my sinuses swell and I blow green into my hankie."

Milton said, "Marlene, we do not discuss the color of residue in our hankie."

"He asked. Anyway, this is the tail end of our Rocky Mountain list. We're going on home tomorrow. Fluff Puff misses her built-in water dish."

I considered a life of running here and there seeing how much you could say you've done without actually doing anything. It seemed uniquely modern. Like the guy with no friends trying to collect as many friends as possible on social media. What my dad used to call bassackwards.

"Have you ever considered looking at the sights on your bucket list?"

"Oh, no," Milton said. "No time for..."

"Lollygagging." Marlene finished his sentence. I got the idea she did that often. "You start savoring experiences you get yourself sidetracked and you never finish your list."

"You die without fulfilling your potential."

"Milton tried once at Grand Canyon, but he got so dizzy he had to drink three Pepsis to calm down."

"We lost most of the afternoon."

"Two hours closer to death and nothing to show for it but Cola burps."

Green residue in the hankie and Cola burps — I was two steps closer to filling in my own bucket list.

They say I should have been here before it got ruined by folks like me.
   − James McMurtry

Here is what kept me from sleeping last night: Bullwhip is a noun and horsewhip is a verb. Why is that?

The whip question came about because I dropped in on Clyde Walsowski-Smith's house and found Clyde's father, Wally, in the kitchen where Clyde was pouring hydrogen peroxide into his dad's ear. Wally's nose was bleeding. He had a scrape over one eye, and, like everyone else who's been beaten up in Jackson Hole, he was writing a letter to the editor.

Wally wanted my help. "Is stump sucker one word or two?"

Clyde said, "I had a stump sucking llama one. Could clean a fence post down to the barbwire in a hour flat."

I poured myself coffee. Clyde drinks what in this area is called Mormon coffee. The stuff is so weak you can drop in a dime and tell whether it's heads or tails there sitting on the bottom of the cup.

"Who's a stump sucker?"

Wally licked the lead on his pencil. "Red Doppelganger. He says Mr. R's Cafeteria was in what's now the Gart Sports parking lot. Anybody with a brain knows it was in the old Bubba's building. When I corrected Red he tried to bite my ear off, like the stump sucker he is."

Clyde said, "Gart turned into Sports Authority ten years ago, Dad."

"I got enough trouble keeping up with the old times. I can't be expected to follow what happened yesterday."

The fight took place at a meeting of TOTS — the True Olds Timers Syndicate. TOTS meets in the sub-sub-basement of the Wort Hotel, so far down the current owners don't even know the room exists, where Wally and his cronies come together to argue about what used to be where and who used to be whom.

As in every tourist town in the world — from Paris, France, to Wall, South Dakota — the definition of what makes a person local is hotly debated by those who are and those who would like to be. It comes down to this: I am a local and anyone who arrived after me is a newbie. Seasonals don't count. People rich enough to hire out the shoveling of their driveways don't count. In certain parts of the county — Hoback Junction and Buffalo Valley — Democrats don't count.

After weeding out everyone who came late or doesn't count, there aren't that many left.

TOTS has a strict definition of *old timers*. An old timer has to have lived through a winter in Jackson Hole before the ski area opened — 1966, although the date is another point of bitter conflict.

"How many old timers are there?" I asked.

Wally said, "Six. Seven if you count Modell Burbank out in Kelly, but we don't count her. Modell borrowed a pickaxe off Henry Widowmeyer in 1961 and didn't return it. The true locals have shunned her ever since."

"Long time to ostracize someone over a pickaxe."

"Modell claims she brought the pick back the day she used it to bury her pet goat Emory. Ever'one knows she ate that goat and never buried her at all."

The first wave of settlers who descended on the valley in the 1880s were basically hippies and survivalists here because there was no law north of Salt Lake. They couldn't stand the second wave who pulled in in the 1920s and built schools and churches and, in the opinion of the way-back old timers, screwed up everything. The end of World War II brought a bunch looking for cheap land, and, at almost the same moment, the opening of Grand Teton Monument chased out as many as it brought in, at first anyway.

The so-called Fourth Epoch of Jackson Hole came when the ski area gave us something to do year-round. Men and women from the other epochs feel vastly superior to the ski bums.

The author Donald Hough was the first to talk about the *Cocktail Hour in Jackson Hole.* Back in his time from Labor Day in September to Memorial Day the end of May there was nothing to do here but drink. That's how the old timers liked it.

"That ski area brought movies and cable TV, and now they've built a Center for the Arts to go with their monster of a parking garage." Wally spit on Clyde's kitchen floor. "What do we need all these winter distractions for? I've seen a heap of changes in this valley the last sixty years and I've fought every one of them."

Wally took Clyde and me over to a meeting in the sub-sub-basement. "Normally, you wouldn't be allowed in, but Red is afraid we'll all die in an earthquake down here and there won't be anyone to record how it used to be."

He gave the secret knock — *quick, quick, slow, slow,* the two-steppers mantra — and we were let into a room furnished exactly like the old Happy Hound. Pine tables swathed in soft lacquer, chairs you stuck to if you sat in them wearing shorts. They had weak coffee and creamers shaped like cows with the artificial whitener dribbling from their open mouths. The sugar envelopes were white. No pink, yellow, or blue packets allowed.

The assembled TOTS were fighting over the difference between a local, an old timer, and a native.

"To be a local you had to have eaten in the Elk Horn between midnight and dawn," Red said. "And survived."

Wally stayed away from Red. His ear was still bleeding.

I asked, "What makes a native."

"Born here over fifty years ago. I've heard high school kids calling themselves natives and whining about how downtown has lost its character. Hasn't been any character on the square since Clover the Killer's last shootout."

"Have you run into Hank Elkrunner lately?" Wally asked. Hank is our token Shoshone. His family has been in and out of the valley for 300 years. "He's been going around with a can of black spray paint, blocking out all the WYOMING NATIVE bumper stickers."

"Why would Hank do such a thing?" I asked.

"The man is a snob. Thinks because his people got here first they're better than the rest of us."

"I can't stand snobs," Red said. "I haven't liked elitists since the park closed the Jenny Lake store in 1962."

"Sixty-four," Wally said.

"Sixty-two."

That's when Red offered to bullwhip Wally with a horse-whip and I scurried off in search of a dictionary.

SUMMER 2015

I took my Letter to the Editor over to St. John's Hospital to show Clyde Walsowski-Smith who was recovering for a hemorrhoid operation, because he spent too much time on a horse. Westerners refuse to post — it's wimpy, like an Englishman riding to the hounds — so, at a trot, our bottoms whack the saddle like clapping hands at a concert. Hard on hemorrhoids.

I found Clyde sitting up in bed in a pain killer fog doing what everyone does in bed these days — reading stuff off his phone.

He looked up at me and said, "Did you know a castrated moose won't drop his antlers come winter."

"I'd rather know how they figured that out."

"I think it was from natural castration causes, like jumping a barbwire fence.

"Even so, I've watched moose through binoculars a lot in my life, and I've never could tell if they were castrated or not."

Clyde peered down at his phone. He said, "Old timers called them Devil's Horns."

"Maybe old timers had nothing better to do than castrate

moose just to see what would happen. Here, read this. It's my Letter to the Editor."

Clyde went into a narcotic nod. I could tell he was faking, he hadn't been nodding before I asked him to read my letter.

"Is it about politics? I don't believe in politics."

"It's about guns."

He looked unhappy. "Even saying the word *gun* in Wyoming can get your bashed. I don't want anything to do with it."

"Read the letter."

Here is my letter.

Dearest Editor,

I have a prediction: When House Bill 114, the "Wyoming Repeal Gun-Free Zones Act" passes, and it will eventually, the Wyoming Cowboys football team will never lose another home game. Imagine you are the Colorado State quarterback and you drop back to zip a pass to your wide receiver in the end zone and you realize that at a minimum, you are surrounded by twenty thousand rabid, screaming fans, in many cases, drunk fans, in some cases, with the impulse control of ten year olds — heck, this is Wyoming, some of them will be ten year olds — and all these insane people are armed to the teeth. Are you going to complete that pass?

My feeling is most of the actual shooting will take place within the stands. You have to remember the Colorado State fans — stoned to the gills on legal marijuana — will also be armed. That shoot-out at the Border War that journalists love to write about will no longer be a metaphor. It will be legal.

The bill also grants those with a permit to carry guns in government buildings, public schools (No more Fs in social studies!), and public events, such as Fourth of July fireworks displays (another 10,000 drunks get-together).

But think Star Valley. Those folks aren't about to pass a local law that infringes on their second amendment rights. Will our basketball team be relaxed knowing everyone in the gymnasium hates their guts for being filthy rich, environmentalists, and what's worse, Democrats, from the despised Teton County? And all these angry yet fine people have guns. Heck, they won't have to shoot us. Just wait till our guard stands at the free throw line and the entire student section behind the basket starts waving semi-automatic weapons — all legal. See if our free throw shooting percentage doesn't go down.

Sadly, this is not satire or paranoid ramblings. I recall a few years ago when a concerned Star Valley mother charged onto the mat at a wrestling match and physically attacked a referee. Now, think what would have happened had she been packing iron. Or the referee had been armed. Or the coaches. The wrestlers on the bench. The opposing teams' parents.

For those of us who enjoy life when it is interesting as opposed to safe, this bill is wonderful news. For the rest of you liberals, I suggest you purchase a sports package from ESPN and stay home.

This bill will make Wyoming famous. It is the best thing we have done since we passed the bill last year making it illegal to teach science in science class.

Clyde looked up from my letter. "Can I have your TV when they shoot you." Clyde covets my flat screen.

"I'm not about to get shot."

"You will if you print this letter. You'll meet the same angel I did when I was coming out of the anesthesia."

This was interesting. Clyde doesn't believe in extra-sensory beings. "You met a real angel?"

He nodded. "A true messenger from God. I never met an angel before. She was pretty."

"Tell me about it."

"They had me by myself in a holding room where they take

you after the operation till you wake up. I opened my eyes before I was supposed to and there she stood, next to my bed."

"How could you tell it was an angel?

"She shimmered with translucent blue skin, white satin bikini, and wings. She carried a walnut case by both hands, like a cigar box. She had on glass slippers."

I said, "Glass slippers is Cinderella, Clyde. Not the Bible."

"It was a vision. I didn't make it up. She glided to my side and whispered, 'That doctor just ripped out your back side.'

"I said, 'Yep.'

" 'Would you care for a replacement.' She opened the box to show me six anuses in velvet slots. Six different sizes and shapes, from the vertical crack with a pencil piercing to an asterisk like Kurt Vonnegut drew in whichever book he drew anuses in. There was also a cross, like cartoonists draw eyes on people who have been knocked silly. And a curl, like a seashell or galaxy. There was another one but it didn't look like anything but a bull's eye.

"The angel crooned, 'Take your pick.'

"I studied them closely, knowing I'd be living the rest of my life with my answer. None were perfect. They just didn't seem like me.

" 'Is this all the choices?'

The angel smiled like, well, like an angel. 'Oh, no,' she said. 'Don't you know, there are an unlimited number of assholes in America.' "

I hit the nurse's button and had them bring Clyde more morphine.

P lease train your bears to be where guests can see them. This was an expensive trip to not get to see bears.

A visitor left that note in the Comments box at one of the hotels in Yellowstone last summer and within two weeks it was all over Facebook, Yahoo, and various social sites where people say snarky things about strangers. None of the hundred of so comments I read thought the tourist was anything other than a sincere idiot.

Having written my share of fake letters to the editor and notes to Congressmen — who do you think gave Scott Walker the idea of building a wall across the northern border to keep out Canadians — I myself was dubious as to the innocence of the Comment card. But what do I know? How can one person figure it out when a million didn't?

Anyway, the note got me thinking. How does Yellowstone position its wildlife for tourist season? There's too much money at stake for the deal to be random. I've seen the same buffalo in the same swampy pond every June for seven summers. And there's a moose down in the willows off the Jackson Lake Lodge back deck. You can watch it through a coin operated tower viewer on a pole, provided by the lodge. That moose hasn't moved a muscle in years. Nature doesn't park an animal and leave it.

Obviously many of the national park animals are animatronic. Ever take the jungle ride at Disneyland? No one over six thinks the hippo is real. Why do people fall for a stuffed wolf on a mountaintop a mile away at Roaring Mountain?

I'm sure you'll be happy to know many of the animals closest to the roads are real. In order to ensure survival through the harsh Yellowstone winter, the government rounds up all the wildlife they can catch and keeps them in heated pens under the hot springs terraces at Mammoth. That's what the hot water is for.

In November I drove to Mammoth to meet my friend Eats the Dirt, the famous Kickapoo buffalo whisperer. Eats the Dirt claims he's in charge of animal placement in Yellowstone. I've never known whether to believe him or not. It seems impossible, but I hate to write off a minority shaman's culture. Kickapoo say they talk to beasts. It's arrogant for white people to dismiss their beliefs.

Bottom line is I can't talk to animals, unless you count being able to read domestic cat moods by their ears.

So, I had to trust Eats the Dirt's translation.

They keep the animals segregated in species specific pens to cut down on the spread of brucellosis and ripping each other to shreds. Eats the Dirt stood at a podium, like a conductor with an orchestra, and directed the meeting where they divvied up the prime locations. It's one of the last places in America where seniority matters.

"Where's Max?"

An ancient by moose years moose lifted his head. Eats the Dirt translated for me. "He said, '*Here.*'

"I want you in that meadow at Beryl Springs. But closer to the road this summer. Tourists are getting blasé about ungulates. They won't slam their brakes for less than carnivores. You can't cause a decent traffic jam 200 yards out in the grass."

"But the feed over by the road is oily from construction trucks. And children throw toys at me. I had ice cream on my horns all last summer. We need a sign says BEARS EAT ICE CREAM. MOOSE DON'T."

"Your job isn't to complain. It's to stop traffic. The hotels pay us to make certain no one sees the whole park in a day. You can't shirk."

"And why do we care about the hotels?"

"Without them making a profit Yellowstone becomes a strip mine. Think where you'd be then. Can't have land not producing cash. I want more elk in the Hayden Valley. You guys are not earning your keep in the back country."

This brought on a chorus of *boos* from the elk. Even I could hear them.

"And you buffalo. I'm moving all six of you who stomped tourists at Old Faithful over to Lamar Valley. Let you dodge wolves for a summer, see if that doesn't make you appreciate our visitors."

The buffalo expressed outrage, which, in a buffalo means a lot of snorting and mucus blowing.

"The fool put a child on my back. Was I supposed to take that lying down?"

"I was surrounded by selfie sticks and flashes went off in my eyes. I charged the phone. Can I help it if a man got in my way? Don't they know we are wild animals?"

Eats the Dirt said, "Breaking tourist legs is bad public relations."

Here's an interesting scientific fact. Since selfies became the fad, buffalo stomps have increased threefold. A tourist group — often foreigners so they can't read the Danger flyers — stand with the backs to the buffalo and aim phones at them. Heck, I would charge if they did it to me.

"At least we didn't kill anybody," the elder female whined. "Grizzlies kill people but you give them the prime locations."

Eats the Dirt's tone was one of a grownup addressing a fractious child. "A grizzly with three cubs can back traffic up four miles. You cause complete chaos like a good bear jam and we'll see about a better location."

"Might happen if you let us mount our cows on the center stripe," said a bull elk who hadn't gotten over his rut yet.

"Sorry," Eats the Dirt said. "We're a family park."

The elder buffalo wouldn't let go of her complaint. "But Blaze ate a health care professional. The government put her to sleep."

A marmot piped up. "They didn't put her to sleep. They killed her."

"And let this be a lesson to you all," Eats the Dirt said. "Blaze wasn't destroyed for killing the guy. She was destroyed for eating him. People have a myth that says once an animal has tasted human flesh he'll never stop killing until the animal is hunted down and exterminated. The story started with Tarzan and spread to Zane Grey. Now all the writers buy it."

"I've eaten human flesh," said a wolf. "Tastes like chicken."

There followed an awkward silence, the animal kingdom version of Don't Ask, Don't Tell.

"Why does the government persist in this *Put to Sleep* balderdash?" asked a sandhill crane. "Do they think we don't know the difference sleep and dead."

Eats the Dirt went into the medicine man voice he uses for explaining deep stuff. The government won't ever say *kill*. They don't know the word."

"But it's all the same," the sandhill said. "Do they think we're stupid?"

"It's a matter of tone. Tone is important."

Eats the Dirt held up his hand and counted off his fingers. "Here's what humans write or say when they mean kill an animal: crop, take, thin, harvest, suppress, put down, put to sleep, subdue, repress, extinguish, censor, localize, secure, limit, check, clear, pacify, reduce, cull, trim, manage, regulate, lose, euthanize and, my favorite, maintain population objectives.

"Not once have I heard a government minion admit to killing an animal."

"That's sick," said a coyote, who was himself the subject of a massive reduction program across the West.

"And those are just some of the terms they use for wiping out animals. They have a whole other set of words for people."

I perked up for this. I'm interested in how people rationalize legal ways of killing other people. It's usually religious, but sometimes they mix in money and sex.

Eats the Dirt said, "You should go online and download some of those Pentagon documents. Do a Find/Replace switching out *Collateral damage* for *Kill innocent bystanders*. See if that doesn't change the tone."

SUMMER 2016

The last time Roger Ramsey and I met for coffee at Pearl Street Bagels he showed me a *Jackson Hole Daily* story about a guy who set a speed record for kayaking the Grand Canyon.

"This kid paddled 277.1 miles in 34 hours, two minutes. Broke the record that was three days old."

I drank coffee. "Why?"

"Why what?"

"Why would someone want to go through the Grand Canyon as quickly as possible? Did this person have time to admire the sunlight on the cliffs or the beauty of a side channel waterfall? I'd think the prize would go to the person slowest through the canyon."

Roger chuckled at my naiveté. "That's not how competition works."

"Can you set a record for appreciating beauty? Speed meditation? Speed eating? There are things that shouldn't be a contest. Dancing, music, mountain climbing, breathing clean air."

"That's not the American way. We have competitive yoga next week at the Center."

"That's goes against the purpose of yoga. Would you give an award for fastest prayer?"

"Last week the World Sign Spinning Championship was held in Las Vegas. The worst job I can imagine would be wearing a bear costume and standing on a corner in 90 degree heat spinning a sign that says ARTHUR'S BAIL BONDS, and yet, even they have a world championship."

"When I was a youth I once completed sex in a second and a half, but I didn't expect a trophy."

Roger got sidetracked by when the stopwatch started and stopped and did I really time the experience.

I said, "She did."

"You should talk to Myron Suggs. He holds the record for the fastest Yellowstone circuit. Three hours and seven minutes, Flagg Ranch to the upper loop and back to Flagg Ranch. In July. Now he owns Yellowstone Speed Tours. Takes clients on a complete vacation in four hours flat."

"And people pay for this?"

"Lots of tourists these days only have a half day to see all there is to see in Yellowstone Park. Myron's their guy."

Later, when I tracked down Myron, he expressed pride at speed travel. He said, "I'd been to the park a thousand times. When they offered me an entry in the Yellowstone Grand Prix, I couldn't pass it up."

"I didn't know Yellowstone has a grand prix."

"It's not publicized. We race in July and we don't always obey speed limits. My commercial trips are four hours instead of three, for safety reasons. No use running over wildlife unless you have to."

"I take it in competition you don't hesitate to create road kill."

Myron shrugged. "No guts, no glory."

"I never heard that saying from a literal standpoint."

"Look," he said. "I'm taking a family up tomorrow. You should ride with us."

We met at 7:45 at Flagg Ranch. Penny and Brick Chisholm along with their five-year-old son, Brick Jr., tourists from Olathe, Kansas, who looked the way you would expect a Brick and Brick Jr. from Kansas to look. Heavy coats over t-shirts advertising a kindergarten casino night with plaid shorts and shoes appropriate for poolside lounging. Penny introduced me to the blue rag Brick Jr. was sucking on.

"His name is Mr. Magoo."

Brick Jr. made a weird noise with his nose. "Mr. Magoo doesn't like you."

"That's okay," I said, "because the real Mr. Magoo is a cartoon character making fun of handicapped people and I don't care for him either."

Myron said, "Let's get started. We have a vacation to replicate before lunch."

We loaded Myron's Chevy Tahoe van. I sat up front with Myron while the Chisholms took the second row of seats. The third row had a cooler, a picnic basket of snacks, and a plastic funnel attached to a hose that ran under the seat and out the bottom of the van. That would be our bathroom.

As we shot toward the South Entrance, Myron explained the rules of the quickie Yellowstone adventure. We had to buy ice cream at Mammoth and the Chisholms had to witness an actual Old Faithful eruption.

"Can't fake Old Faithful on a screen like you can wolves," Myron said. "I'd lose my guide license."

We powered up the Lewis River Canyon at sixty, blowing through a bus tour from Taiwan. Selfie sticks scattered like antelope hit by a tornado.

"How do you time Old Faithful? I asked. "Seems like you barely miss it, you'll lose an hour."

"There's an app." Myron steered with one had and leaned over to show me his phone. "Old Faithful Eruption Predictor. $1.95 at your app store. More accurate than the Park Service."

He thumb clicked the geyser icon. "She'll go off at 11:22. We should hit it, if we make haste."

Our first major obstacle came leaving West Thumb when we charged up behind a Winnebago with a MY OTHER VEHICLE IS A WHEEL CHAIR bumper sticker going twenty miles an hour. Myron flipped a switch than turned on one of those high volume European sirens — WAH—*eeee*—WAH — scaring the wadding out of the codger at the wheel. He froze dead in the right lane and we flew around.

Brick Jr. whined. "Mr. Magoo has to go pee."

Myron didn't slow down. "Use the funnel behind you. We don't have time for pit stops."

"Mr. Magoo can't go pee in a funnel."

Myron used his soothing crazy tourists voice. "Your parents won't tell you, Brick boy, so I will. Mr. Magoo is a rag."

Brick Jr. burst into sobs and Penny Chisholm told Myron he had no business destroying her son's childhood.

"It isn't like I told him the truth about Santa Claus," Myron said.

Brick Jr. snuffled. "What truth?"

Brick Sr. lit a cigar. "Pretty day, ain't it?"

Myron said, "You'll have to look at your phone to be sure. I wouldn't trust outside."

I think we clipped a moose on Dunraven Pass. I'm not sure.

Penny said, "I'd like to see the moose."

Myron said, "Too late. You can download out of focus photos on my web site. Nobody will know you didn't take it."

Myron used the European siren on a buffalo herd that stampeded over a motorcycle club from Felt, Idaho, on their way to Sturgis. Harleys crunched like Fritos at a nacho bar.

At Mammoth, Myron told the Chisholms to wait in the van for ice cream. "Secret is don't let them out," he said. "That woman would disappear in the Ladies and we'd never leave." We bought Rocky Road all around because it was softest — quickest to scoop.

The Old Faithful app ($1.95, don't forget) said we had 32 minutes to make Old Faithful or it would go off without us. By Norris, the Chisholm family was too terrified to finish their ice creams. I had to pass a trash bag.

A flag man stood before a line of cars a half mile long outside Madison Junction. Myron tore up the wrong side of the highway, pulled in front of the front of the line, rolled down his window, and held out a fifty dollar bill.

The flagman said, "Go on through, sir. You'll have to hurry to catch the pilot car."

We careened around the Old Faithful cloverleaf with 90 seconds to spare. Myron whipped into an Employees Only driveway that cut around the side of the lodge just as Old Faithful erupted.

"There she blows!" Myron shouted. "You folks want to stay for the whole thing?"

Brick Jr. whined. "I can't see."

"Get out and stand by the van. You can see it through those people."

This infuriated Brick Sr. "You didn't tell us we'd have to leave the vehicle."

Penny said, "There's bears out there. I'm not going outside and neither is my son."

"Suit yourself." Myron popped the top off a Red Bull and we watched Old Faithful while the Chisholms squinched down to see out the front window.

We hit Flagg Ranch with two minutes to spare.

Myron turned around in his captain's chair. "There you go. The four hour Yellowstone tour."

Brick Jr. wailed. *"Mr. Magoo!"*

Brick Sr. asked, "Where did you see him last?"

"He hid in the pee funnel at the ice cream place."

This brought on more wailing and teeth gnashing while Myron crawled under the van to see if Mr. Magoo got caught in the exit hose.

"Nope, folks. It's extra wide in case of number twos. Mr. Magoo is long gone."

More screams. More recriminations.

Penny Chisholm took a stand. "We have to go back."

That's when I said, "I'll be getting out now."

WINTER 2016

We live with a three-legged turtle named Waldo who only eats worms so once every month or so I have to buy worms. Those of you who don't live on the Lycra Archipelago — Sun Valley, Jackson Hole, Steamboat Springs, Aspen, Park City, Taos — won't understand what a pickle this puts me in.

Political correctness in Jackson isn't refusing to open doors for old women or keeping up with the correct way to address diversities, it's how you catch fish. In order of proper through acceptable to shameful, the list goes like this: 1) dry flies with barbless hooks, 2) nymphs, 3) spinners, 4) fish eggs and stink bait, and down there under the pond scum, we find 5) worms. Except for a few truly warped chinless wonders dabbling in electric currents or explosives, worm fishermen are the lowest of the low.

If any of my peer group at Trout Unlimited caught me buying worms I would be stripped of my Prius. Banned from Tevas. Shunned at the Whole Grocers bulk bins.

They're for my turtle won't wash. No one is going to buy that any more than they will *I got it from the toilet seat.*

In October, Waldo slurped the last of his worms. I tried a basil reduced hummus lump — no soap. He craned his neck out at a piece of cantaloupe and bit my finger. The turtle is on a macrobiotic worm diet. He rather die than eat commercial turtle chow.

First, I approached Heather Heidi Walsowski-Smith's grandson Romy and offered him five dollars if he'd make my purchase. He said sure but only if I'd buy him a six-pack of Blue Ribbon.

I said, "How old are you, kid?"

"Fifteen."

I gave him my responsible adult look.

He said, "Fourteen, but I'm mature."

"Your mother would scalp me. I could go to jail. You don't go to jail for buying worms."

Romy was too smart for words. "If those doctors and Realtors at Rotary find out you have a refrigerator full of worms you'll never eat Sunday Brunch in this valley again."

So I went to Browse and Buy and bought a blonde wig and a Rock Springs cheerleading sweater with LaDonna stitched on the breast, a white pleated skirt, and red trainers. I would have shaved my legs if the sweater hadn't said Rock Springs.

I parked two blocks from Stone Drug and walked over. By the time I arrived, I'd collected a pack of six dogs and a tame raven.

The worms are in a mini-refrigerator up front, by the door. My plan was to get in and out in ninety seconds. No one back in Sporting Goods and Licenses would know I'd been in the building.

Of course, Penny Wilkerson at the cash register flipped that toggle that turns on the loud speakers. *"Price check on night crawlers!"*

I could have throttled Penny only it might get me in the paper Police Blotter.

WORM FISHERMAN THROTTLES INNOCENT CASHIER

I flashed back on high school, buying condoms that would

never get used. I slid into Rexall and put on my deep radio DJ voice.

"Prophylactics, if you please."

And Harriet Gardner yelled that Price Check line for the whole store to hear. Took me five years to realize Harriet did that every time a kid came in for rubbers.

"Price check on Trojans. I assume you want small?"

Harriet knew the price. She did it to give us a hard time.

Then she said, "You're Liz Sandlin's boy, aren't you. I play contract bridge with Liz on Thursdays."

Why are locals so judgmental about fishing technique anyway? Wyoming used to be the Not My Business What You Do State. Different strokes for different folks. People could be as weird as a carnivorous cow and no one cared so long as you didn't try to convert them. Now, it's "If you don't do things my way, you're dirt."

Lord knows what would happen to a man who kept a few fish for supper. I recently saw a bumper sticker that said CATCH AND RELEASE OR DEATH.

These are the same people who gave me crap when they heard my four year old had never skied from the top of the tram.

"She prefers Casper."

"Child abuser!"

Or the old codger who invited me to run from the Stagecoach to the top of Teton Pass. I'm in my 60s, for Chrissake. In Alabama men my age don't leave the Barcalounger.

But in Jackson Hole, what I got was, "Wimp. Why not spare us your presence and check into a nursing home."

I'm sick of it. Time to come clean. I've lived here 55 years and I deserve to live the way I want to live. No more shame.

I don't go ecstatic for mountain bikes.

I would rather not sleep on the ground.

I cross country ski in Levi's 501s.

I bought my winter boots at K Mart. And they aren't Sorrels.

I eat boxed macaroni and cheese (nothing cheaper than Kraft).

Not all the white sugar I buy goes into hummingbird food.

I prefer lettuce to kale.

Just last month I threw #1 plastic into the #2 plastic bin and when I realized my error I didn't crawl in after it. (This is a double sin since some of my neighbors will be aghast that I owned any #1 plastic in the first place.)

Worst of all — right from the beginning, I was for Hillary over Bernie.

There you have it. Crucify me if you must.

Bottom line: I came out of Stone Drug in my cheerleading outfit, clutching my plastic bag, and that vengeful little turd Romy clicked my photo on his I6. Slapped that picture on Snap Chat with the caption TIM SANDLIN HAS WORMS.

I'm looking to move to South Carolina.

SUMMER 2017

My first encounter with the international No SQUATTING sign was in the national park outhouse at Kelly Warm Springs. This outhouse is something of a destination bathroom. If the Four Seasons had privies the Warm Springs john is what they would look like.

There next to PLEASE DON'T DUMP TRASH DOWN THE HOLE IT IS HARD TO GET OUT was a figure in a circle with a slash across the middle — universal language for *Don't*. In the circle a stick figure squatted, his (or her) feet planted on both sides of the commode.

I knew what the symbol meant because I've been to China and seen the opposite sign. DON'T SIT ON OUR TOILET. Some of the higher end hotels have segregated potty sections — four squats and two sits. Always more squats than sits. Let Americans wait in line if they can't balance like a Thanksgiving balloon over Macy's.

What I don't know is why the Park cares. Besides seat splatter and footprints on the porcelain, what does it matter how people go? I mean, this is an outhouse.

So I drove up to Park headquarters in Moose to find out only to discover there's a new Trump rule against the Park

Information Officer giving out information. I shuffled from office to office, most of the bureaucrats afraid to even tell me what office to go to next. When I asked a secretary where the water fountain was, she ran off.

Finally, I found a man we'll call Larry Langtree because that's not his name. Larry was willing to leak commode policy.

He said, "They break them."

"Who's they?"

"Asian tourists. They stand on the rims and the rims splinter down the middle. We replaced over 20 commodes last summer. Why would a woman stand on the toity to pee?"

"They squat and it's a cultural deal. In China they think we're disgusting for sitting with our bum touching the wet surface where someone else's bum has been."

"Yeah, well no wonder the seat gets wet, if you hover like a helicopter filling a hot tub."

"Once you leave the Chinese cities a lot of the toilets are holes in the floor with yellow stenciled footprints on both sides to show you which way to face, and they have a gallon bucket for soiled toilet paper. They don't allow toilet paper in those small town toilets."

Larry Langtree made a face I would call thoughtful as he worked out the nuances. He said, "We've had a 30 percent rise in Asian bus tours the last two years. They flood the valley in April and May when the tour operators can get cheap room rates."

"Do the operators tell their clients the only days it doesn't rain in May are the days it snows?"

Larry kind of chuckled. "I've seen waves of umbrellas and selfie sticks in front of the elk horn arches. There'll be even more this summer unless Trump starts a war with China."

"Trade or literal?

Larry went furtive on me. "I'm not allowed to say."

Herman Walsowski-Smith, Heather Heidi's grandson, wrote

his master's thesis at Grand Canyon University on tourist toilets the world over. I drove by to see him.

"My favorites are those space ship things in Paris." He showed me a photograph. "After every use they self-clean. There's a sign in front says UNACCOMPANIED CHILDREN UNDER TEN MAY DROWN. Imagine an American can that kills kids. There would be a social media firestorm."

As I admired his portfolio, I felt especially close to the outhouses. "When I was a kid I was scared of outhouses. I knew I'd fall down the hole and never be seen again."

Herman said, "Statistically, you're more likely to be bitten by spiders or rats coming up than you falling down."

"That's a comfort." I pointed to the red stenciled footprints on either side of the hole in a concrete floor. "Is this China?"

"France," Herman said. "In France they call these Turkish water closets. The rest of Europe calls them French thrones. Look at this thermochromatic wall urinal."

It was a two by four in front of a colorful wall with a gutter running at the base. Herman said, "The wall is heat sensitive so when you go on it the colors pulsate and change. You can draw cartoons."

"What's your favorite toilet story?"

Herman considered. "Right here. In Jackson. Do you know the story of Penny Wort?"

"This is true, right? Not fake news."

"Totally true. Charlie Craighead did the research. His cousin Karen and her friend Julia were driving from the Village to Moose and they stopped at the Wort Hotel to use the bathroom."

"When was this?"

"Winter of 1967. Julie heard weird gurgles in the next stall and when that woman left, Julie checked it out and found a newborn baby in the toilet."

"Ish."

"Julie ran out to get cocktail waitresses who fished the baby out and took her to the hospital where they named her Penny Wort. No one ever discovered the birth mother.

"Penny was adopted by a couple in Kansas, got a new name, then went to work in Florida where the eerie part of the story happens."

"The eerie part wasn't being born in a Wort toilet?"

"This part is even more unlikely. By then her name was Wendi. Wendi met and fell in love with a man from Moose, Wyoming. She married him. What are the odds? They live in North Carolina."

My brain went Twilight Zone. How many men grew up in Moose? Twelve, maybe.

"Okay, Herman, that's a bizarre story, but what I need to know, what my readers need to know, is why are the stenciled toilet hole footprints yellow in China but in France they are red?"

Herman closed his portfolio. "Kind of self-evident, don't you think."

"Not to me."

"It's so Keith Richards can tell what continent he's peeing on."

WINTER 2017

Life in Jackson Hole last summer was dominated by the upcoming eclipse. Every conversation for months centered on the run-up — not so much the eclipse itself as the prediction that a Woodstock-sized horde would descend on the valley, consuming our food, water, gasoline, parking spaces, and toilet paper, stripping our town the way Mormon crickets strip a field of sugar beets.

Rumors ran rampant. I heard urban motorcycle gangs would bathe in the Home Ranch sinks, geriatrics in Winnebagos would squat on every inch of asphalt, wolves and badgers would go insane and attack females having their time of month, bats would go blind and fly into satellite dishes, cell phones would only work in Russian, Jesus would rise from Flat Creek.

Anyone with a screen and a squeegee designed a hole-in-the-middle t-shirt. Eclipse beer, wine, bagels, shot glasses, flower arrangements, disposable diapers, TED talks — we sold them all. Every Porta Potty in the intermountain west was hauled to the Hole. While most of us recall August 21, 2017, as the miracle of the moon swallowing the sun, park employees call it the Day of the Great Outhouse Shortage.

My friend Roger Ramsey sold 15,000 pairs of eclipse glasses, then when the market saturated, he jumped on social media to start the rumor of counterfeit glasses that would make you blind, and he sold another 5,000 pairs to people who already owned them.

The weirdest rumor — besides two weddings, a mass L.A. funeral home ashes spreading, and an outdoor Caesarian during totality — was that the Mount Moran Harmonic Convergence Club planned to sacrifice barnyard birds in the belief that it would bring nine nuns who died in a plane crash on Mount Moran in 1950 back to life. As the club slit the domestic fowls throats, the nuns would glissade down Skillet Glacier.

Almost immediately, a second rumor kicked in that a group known as Chickens Matter would kidnap the sacrifices and turn them loose in the Gros Ventre Wilderness where they would form the Clan of the Chicken.

Somehow Roger discovered MMHCC was camped with their cages of grain fed chickens in the Atherton Creek Campground. On the morning of the eclipse we hit the road early to drive out and watch, on the theory that dead nuns would be the eclipse icing on the cake.

The predictions of gridlock in town were worth less than predictions for the World Series in 2056. Broadway was dead, Cache Street deserted. The fear tactics had worked. Locals either got out of town or stayed home. A hundred thousand tourists hunkered in place for fear the other hundred thousand would drive in circles.

It wasn't until we entered Grand Teton that we found the throngs. The Park Service had turned the right lane of the Antelope Flats Loop into a parking lot. The left lane was bumper to butt with cars searching for a spot to land. Each and every one of the hundred outhouses had a lengthy line. No one wanted to spend totality in the potty.

The upshot was Roger and I didn't make Atherton Creek till the eclipse had already started. There we found the cultists and the chicken protectors in a face off. The prospect of violence would have been palpable had both sides not been wearing eclipse glasses. Little cardboard multi-colored eclipse glasses give one the aspect of a praying mantis. Nazi frat brothers in eclipse glasses couldn't frighten a flamingo.

Even in goggles, I recognized Meadow Morningstar, leader of Chickens Matter, and Phoenix Rising, First Facilitator of the Mount Moran Harmonic Convergence Club. Except in their attitudes toward slitting bird throats, the two women have much in common. They're both vegan Bikram hot yoga instructors who wouldn't buy Monsanto bottled water if their lives were at risk.

Of course, they hate each other.

Meadow got right in Phoenix's face and shouted, *"Chickens are people too. They love. They have children. They feel pain."* Behind her five CMers chanted, *"Thou shalt not desecrate poultry."*

Phoenix didn't shout. She formed her fingers into Om air holes and whispered, "We love our chickens."

"So you kill them?"

"Our sacred birds give their beingness so others may achieve eternal life."

Roger said, "Eternal life is better than dead nuns on Moran. Sign me up."

Phoenix gave him a look of disdain. "The nuns will have eternal life. Not us." She turned back to Meadow. "And how long will your free chickens last in the wilderness. The coyotes will declare a feast day."

Meadow said, "The coyotes will see the higher plane in our chickens' hearts and protect them. The lion shall lie with the lamb."

I said, "You're both interesting, but nuts."

At my words, the temperature dropped fifteen degrees. Imagine the most beautiful sunset you've ever seen only it's on all four sides of the horizon. The shadow swept toward us.

One of the Harmonics said, "Totality is nigh," and we all

stared at the sky. For the first time in my life, hype undersold reality.

The corona, the spires and loops, snakes in the pavement, beads, dancing plasma, darkness in the day.

Roger, normally God's own cynic, said, "I knew it would be cool, but I never dreamed it would be this cool."

Meadow wept. Phoenix's crew dropped to their knees. Night fell, first with Venus and Mercury visible, then an array of stars. The chickens roosted and slept. Bats swooped over the campground. Coyotes howled.

Phoenix and Meadow swept into each others arms.

All along a sixty-mile swath of America, everyone of every opinion looked at the same thing and marveled. Even now, weeks later, I haven't met anyone who saw totality who is blasé about it, even teenagers.

A couple minutes later, the diamond ring appeared on the upper right side of the moon, dawn filtered to light. Up on the highway, we heard howls, not of coyotes, but of blown away crowds.

I said, "You forgot to kill your chickens."

Phoenix said, "That was better than immortality. The nuns can wait."

Roger said, "I'm giving all the money I made on glasses to Bill Nye the Science Guy."

I said, "Let's not go overboard."

Then the CMers pulled out their high protein sweet and salty maple trail mix and the sides who were enemies before the eclipse came together over organic oatmeal and nuts.

SUMMER 2018

Some call it a blessing, some a curse, and the oldest of the old-timers say, "It is what it is," which means nothing to me. But the truth of living in the Lycra Archipelago — Jackson Hole, Sun Valley, Steamboat Springs, Aspen, Taos, a few smaller islands of cool — is that you get more company than folks who live in Amarillo. Paradise is nicer to visit than the Home of the Golden Sandies.

After careful study of these visitors, I have broken them into two groups — people you know and people you don't know.

People you know are more welcome when it comes to sleeping on my couch, but even then, some summers they come in waves.

Last June, Cora Ann's nephew Lloyd and three of his buddies crowded into the guest room for a week and a half. They had worked like Millennial mice for 50 weeks and were ready to cut loose. The boys installed a keg on Cora Ann's Pilates table. The vaped in the bathroom. They posted our address on Instagram with the caption COME ON DOWN.

Then they flew off to jobs in various states with legal marijuana. Kids these days make career choices based on personal values.

The very airplane Lloyd left on brought in Lucy Munn, Cora Ann's college roommate from 30 years past. Unlike Lloyd and his derelicts, who kept us awake all night but were basically self-entertaining, Lucy expected quality companionship. Lucy and her husband, Rich, slept all morning, hiked in the afternoon while Cora Ann and I worked, then at five Lucy and Rich were ready for us to eat, drink, and dance ourselves into a high altitude frenzy.

Rich bragged, "I never saw a bar yet I couldn't close."

Cora Ann and I held our own until Lucy and Rick left and my cousin Josh flew in. Josh owns Day Care Air, a commuter service for children of bi-coastal joint custody divorce settlements. Licensed pre-school teachers for flight attendants. Pilots dressed as Disney Princess characters. Josh is fabulously well to do.

Cora Ann and I took Josh to Yellowstone and everyone knows how relaxing that is in summer. Josh rented a houseboat and met a bevy of Lake Hotel cabin maids. We ended up in more a babysitting capacity than fellow rabble-rousers.

Next up was Wynn Powers who worked with us at Signal Mountain Lodge 32 years ago, which, in his eyes, makes us next of kin. Wynn brought a bottle of diet pills so he wouldn't have to rest on his vacation.

"I can sleep at home," Wynn said. "You want to run up Snow King for the sunrise, then we can mountain bike Curtis Canyon and hunt rabbits with our bare hands. I'll show you how the Arapaho barbecue bunny. It takes a tequila marinade."

After that came eclipse week. Imagine a polyester and Cabelas Woodstock.

These were guests we more or less knew. The other kind are cat hair in the back of your throat irritating.

Thursday before Labor Day, a couple who could have jumped out of a 1956 Oldsmobile advertisement showed up on our porch. The woman sported a genuine beehive do the color of Pepto Bismol. The man wore Scot's tartan pants — red and black checks — and a paisley pink shirt with a dickie that blue your toe turns when you stub it hard enough the nail breaks off.

The man flipped his cigarette butt into my lilacs. "Is this the residence of Cora Ann Pym?"

I was all set to say, "I've never heard that name in my life," when Cora Ann came out of the kitchen, drying her hands.

"That's me."

The woman said, "We are George Singleton and Mrs. George Singleton. We go to church with your parents back in Velma Alma."

George said, "We just love Franny and Walt."

Cora Ann said, "My parents' names are Delores and Peter."

"Right. We just love them to pieces. Your mama makes the best pecan casserole in Chickasaw County." The guy pronounced *pecan* like he was from Florida and not Oklahoma where Velma Alma is.

He went on. "They were at our house for hand-cranked pawpaw ice cream and watermelon Sunday and Petey said he would snatch us bald-headed if we came all this way and didn't drop in on his baby daughter."

I said, "Tell Petey he doesn't have to snatch you. You dropped by," and started to shut the door. George was too fast for me. He stuck a pack of Larks in the crack so the door wouldn't close.

George said, "We called the motel and the woman there said they was full and so's ever'body else. We don't want to bother you none but your daddy said if we ran into a difficult spot you might put us up for a night."

Mrs. George said, "Or two."

Cora Ann looked at me and said, "The guest room is taken but they could have Charlie's bed and we could put him in a tent."

"We don't want to make a fuss," Pink Beehive Woman said.

George said, "Honeybun, go out to the car and get the kids, and make sure both dogs do their business before you bring them in. You know how nervous Flim Flam gets around strangers."

I said, "Flim Flam?"

Roger Ramsey recently introduced me to a secret society that meets deep in the bowels of the Center for the Arts, so far underground even the folks who run the Center don't know it exists.

"The Center doesn't have a basement," I said.

"That's what the Nonprofit Tribe thinks," Roger said.

He took me to an elevator and stuck a tiny key like my sister used to use to lock her diary in the slot for emergency opening of stuck doors. I've found people hate being trapped in elevators. It's a pet peeve. Then Roger punched the #3 knob twice and the fan switch off/on. Instead of rising, we went down.

I said, "That's not likely."

Roger said, "You ain't seen the interesting part yet."

The doors opened on a long hallway painted hospital bland that, far as I could surmise, ran under Cache. At the end we came to a green door with a key code box that played musical notes when you poked buttons. Roger punched in the opening to *Also Sproch Zarathustra,* quite loud. Think *2001* loud.

A slot opened.

Roger said, "Swordfish."

The door opened. We were greeted by an elderly woman in

an electric wheelchair, Coast Guard camouflage, and Nike Air Jordans. She said, "You're late, Pilgrim."

Roger said, "I got stuck at Pilates," which I knew as a total lie. He'd been in Pearl Street Bagels all afternoon working Snap Chat.

We crossed an empty way and went through another door — this one Coke can red — into a room where twenty or so people sat on those cheap folding chairs you usually find in a Church annex. Each chair had IDS in white lipstick on the back.

Roger got me a cup of rancid instant coffee. They had artificial creamer in what looked like a tennis ball tube. The flakes floated like dandruff on an oil slick. It tasted okay.

A man in a Century 21 gold blazer with a comb over that could have bedded down a guinea pig stood at the podium. He gripped the podium with both hands.

"Hello, my name is Gordo Gallafalusia and," he paused, "I am not a skier."

A gasp flitted across the room, even though I discovered later that's how all their talks began.

Gordo was so earnest it hurt my eyes to look at him.

"I was born in Jackson Hole. All my life I have lived with the shame. I simply do not enjoy sliding down. I must have been born with this flaw."

The audience nodded and a woman with a beehive under a bike helmet sang, *"Amen."*

Gordo was on a roll. "He tried to hide it, but I saw the disappointment in my father's eyes. I have lost countless summertime companions come the first snow. My wife left me for a half pipe obsessive."

The crowd sighed in support. The Amen lady would have married him on the spot.

He held his arms out like Jesus in a Nazarene painting. "Now, I have found this place and you sheltering, protective friends. I feel safe here, for the first time. I have worth. Dignity. I am proud to belong to IDS."

As the crowd broke into cheers, I leaned toward Roger.

"What?"

He said, "I Don't Ski."

The next few speakers talked along the same lines. A woman dry wall installer had to stop work and home school her kids because of the relentless bullying at school.

"You mama don't do bumps. Nonnie nonnie poo poo."

This brought back memories of my own daughter who came home in tears because she was the only child in first grade who hadn't jumped off the top of the tram.

"I'm never going outside in winter again," she sobbed into my shoulder. "I'm joining the chess club."

"Wow, it's like discovering the extended family I never knew I'd lost," I mumbled to Roger.

"I knew this would be your sanctuary."

Then they had a seminar in Keeping Your Secret.

The leader gave a typical skier line and we had to come up with the response that wouldn't cause ostracization.

"Shred the gnar."

"Send it!" we all shouted except for a front row Rastafarian who yelled *"Sick."*

"The Crags is death cookies and rot."

"Mashed potatoes on the Head Wall!"

"The bomber ripped down bulletproof where a gaper had pulled a yard sale. The bomber caught an edge on a trust fund bunny and cartwheeled into eternity."

The crowd was momentarily stumped. A famous poet said, "Oh."

An artist said, "Woke."

This irritated the leader no end. "Wyoming has a law against anybody over fourteen saying, 'Woke.' You say 'Woke' at the office and your co-workers will kick you off the Secret Santa list for life."

I knew the answer. I stood up and shouted, *"Eat chowder, Spore!"*

"That is correct," Century 21 man said. "You can never go wrong with *Eat chowder.*"

As the meeting broke up and we lined up at the buffet table to load our compostable paper plates with Teenie Weinies and Velveeta-filled celery sticks arranged around a gravy boat full of ranch dressing, Roger said, "How did you know about the 'Eat chowder'?"

I poured myself an NPR giveaway mug of kombucha. "That's what my wife says when I leave the toilet lid up at night."

"Eat chowder, Spore?"

"I'm not sure what Spore means. I'm afraid to ask."

SUMMER 2019

On a beautiful spring afternoon Delores and I lounged about our favorite independent coffee shop, enjoying our latte and chai, inventing tales based on the lives of the tourists in line — that one has a You Tube pod cast on macramé window coverings. You can tell just by looking at her. — when a woman in ski boots and what in my youth was called a car coat crashed through the door with the word, *"Idiot."*

I assume she was talking to someone outside, but who knows. She wore enough turquoise to win the Georgia O'Keefe lookalike contest and carried a brown pug in a sling, like the Nez Perce used for babies back in fur trading times.

The woman charged over to the only empty table and slapped down her cell phone before she went to stand in line. This is the worst social blunder one can commit in Wyoming, right up there with posthole walking on a cross-country ski track.

The guy at the head of the line, who'd just gotten his drink, looked at the phone and sighed, no doubt wishing he was from New York or Paris, any place where it would be normal to raise a stink. Instead, he went outside to sit on the curb.

Delores nodded at the phone on the empty table. "In Singapore that's called *Kiasu*. It's a trait they admire."

"Cheating is admired?"

"Getting a competitive edge is good no matter how you do it. Women carry packets of tissues to stake out a table in the food court before they order."

"That would get your tissues blown on and tossed here. I'm surprised no one has taken her phone to the front and turned it into the lost and found."

"Wyomingites are too aloof to mess with someone else's stuff. That phone could sit there three days and no one would touch it."

By then Angry Woman had worked her way to the head of the line where she took the pug out of his sling and plopped him on the counter where he commenced to snuffling up the pastry samples.

The woman more or less shouted. "Hashtag, remember your gluten intolerance."

Kimberly Sue Matson was working the counter. Kimberly Sue has a PhD from Duke in kinesiology. Like so many others, she came to Jackson to ski and hasn't quite left.

Kimberly moved the samples plate back to her work shelf. "It's not dog food either."

"You don't have to snap."

"Why not?"

The woman oozed a huge sigh and said, "Deal with it," which is my least favorite saying, except maybe, "If I don't do somebody else will." We all have our peeves.

The woman went on before Kimberly could snap out a pithy comeback. "Just make me a half caff, hazelnut, triple shot, no foam, extra hot cappuccino."

Kimberly might have fixed the concoction for a polite customer. For this woman doing her best Sean Penn imitation — no way.

"I'm sorry, ma'am, but we have a four-adjective policy. I'm not allowed to do five. You'll have to drop one demand."

The woman's face changed color. Imagine moving from the top half of a tequila sunrise to the bottom half. "What are you, stupid? You're paid minimum wage to give me what I ask for."

Which isn't true, by the way. Jackson Hole's baristas are the top of the service industry pecking order.

To her credit, Kimberly didn't play the Duke doctorate card. "I can put together any four-adjective drink your little heart desires."

"This is why you work in an apron and I work in Hermès."

"Lady, order or move along."

"Okay. A pumpkin Frappuccino. Is that simple enough for you?"

"This isn't Starbucks. We don't Frap."

The pug lifted his squatty back leg and tinkled on the cookie display.

The woman exploded at Kimberly. "Now, look what you've done."

"I didn't pee on the counter."

"You made Hashtag nervous. He has an irritable urethra. He loses control when people criticize me."

Delores had had enough. She snatched the phone off the empty table and strode to the counter.

"Somebody lost their phone, Kimberly. Can I keep it?"

The woman snarled. "You know very well that's mine. I left it to claim my rightful table."

"We don't do that in Wyoming. You must be from Boston."

That one hit home. The woman snapped from self-righteous rage to self-righteous self-pity. "I'll have you know, I'm a local."

"No, you're not," Kimberly said. "You're a second home owner."

The coffee shop hushed. The only sound was the high wheeze from Hashtag's lungs.

Kimberly went for the kill. "You come six weeks in the summer and one in winter and think you own the valley."

The woman sucked back tears. "I deserve to get my way. I contribute to 122 nonprofits. I sit on three boards. I compost regularly."

I decided it was time to get involved. I moved into the center of the action and said, "Composting is a credit to your species."

She looked at me gratefully. "Thank you, kind sir."

"People think because you're filthy rich you don't have feelings." I tutted sympathetically. "I'd bet anything you have feelings."

Delores snorted.

The woman sniffed. "I have more feelings than most upper middle class career women."

I put my arm around her shoulders. "Why don't you step over here and tell me about yourself. Kimberly, would you pour this old dear a cup of black coffee?"

The woman made a sound similar to a hedge fund baby snorting white powder off the back of a toilet. "Can I have room for cream?"

Kimberly said, "Not till she cleans up the dog pee."

Hashtag sniffed my hand on the woman's shoulder. He bit me.

For some reason known only to God and Nostradamas Roger Ramsey scored the job of playing Santa Claus at Teton Village. Why the anti-toddler would let himself be kicked in the shins by children in ski boots is a mystery to those who know him.

My theory is his wife, Maurey, demanded retribution for a serial social blunder Roger committed at last summer's company barbecue. It must have been a doozy for Roger to don the Merry Costume and sit on a snow bank molded throne (with a side table for his tequila slurpie) there behind the Mangy Moose.

Roger didn't don the entire Merry Costume. Just the top half since the original trousers were large enough to hide a microwave oven in the seat. Roger wore orange snow pants from Dick's Sporting Goods — the sort with the barf-resistant bib — and Tony Lama cowboy boots. The top half was straight Santa red velvet, lily white faux fur trimming, and a beard that smelled like cat box on account of where it is stored the rest of the year.

I rode the START bus out to the Village to document

Roger's original Grinch act for Instagram. Somebody had to. These days an action isn't real if there's no image of it.

I arrived as a little girl ran off, weeping, her mother screeching about a formal complaint.

Roger drank slurpie and called to the retreating figures. "The prom is over, lady. Tell your kid it's a rough world."

The next little boy to climb aboard was five or so and clothed in six layers of Gor Tex.

Roger said, "You're sticky."

The kid said, "You smell."

"Why are you sticky?"

The lad licked the gaps between his fingers. "Rhonda June showed me how to make ice cream from snow and Karo syrup."

"You can't do that anymore. Snow turned radioactive in the 70s, and who is Rhonda June?"

"My au pair." The kid pointed to a girl facing away so she wouldn't have to watch the child she was watching. Rhonda June had porpoise pod sleeve tattoos and more piercings than Saint Sebastian.

The kid asked Santa for a pair of Stockli Stormrider Pro skis. I Googled quickly and saw where they sell for a bit under $500.

Roger said, "You'll outgrow them in six months."

The kid said, "What is your point, Santa Claus?"

Roger spread his knees and the kid went down like hung man falling through a trap door. At his scream, Rhonda June oozed over to pick him out of the snow.

She said, "Smooth move, Ex Lax."

Roger said, "Where did you find Karo syrup in Jackson Hole?"

Next boy was older. He had a list on his IPad. "Uglydoll Swarovski watch, Makeblock mBot Smart Robot kit, KD Interactive Aura Drone with Glove Controller, Lego Hogwarts Castle, Tom Clancy's Six: Siege," which I think is an Xbox thing.

"And I demand a Nintendo 3DS, the same one Justin Bieber endorsed in his 'All I Want for Christmas Is You' video with Mariah Carey."

Roger was almost but not quite speechless. I'd call him flabbergasted. He finally got out, "Is your name Trump?"

The kid went haughty. Six year olds can nail haughty. "My name is Xerxes. Write that in your book. Two Xs."

Roger pretended to look for his book. Was he supposed to have a book? "Look Xerxes with two Xs. I decide who is naughty and who is nice and you are naughty at a bizarre level. For Christmas, I'm bringing you two Mandarin oranges and a #2.5 lead pencil, and if you don't pass them on to the less fortunate –"

"Which is everybody," Xerxes said.

"You won't get squat next year either."

Xerxes made a production of taking Roger's picture on his IPad. "Okay, *Santa,* my dad can buy and sell the North Pole. In point of fact, he already has. When he gets through with you you'll be living in a cardboard box in Myanmar, selling match sticks to monks."

Roger said, "In point of fact, get off my snow bank."

A small girl with red curls and a Greta Thunberg sweatshirt two-foot hopped onto Santa's lap, spilling some of Roger's slurpie. She asked for an end to environmental degradation.

Roger said, "You got it. What else?"

"Red flag background checks for wife abusers buying AR-15s."

"I can do that. Anything more?"

The girl reached up and yanked on Roger's white collar. "How many polar bears died so you could look like a Coca Cola commercial?"

My take is Roger was nonplussed. "This is polyester."

"Plastic."

"I don't know what polyester is, kid — "

"It's plastic, like your straw."

"If you'd rather I kill a polar bear than wear fake fur that can be arranged."

"Either way, the Santa Claus paradigm is a metaphor for the destruction of the Artic."

An LED-like light came on in Roger's eyes. Something CLICKED.

"You're a ringer, aren't you, little girl? Somebody put you up to this."

He stared my way. I shrugged. "Wasn't me."

Roger blasted on. "No end of depredation for you. No red flag checks of wife beaters. I'm bringing you a lump of soft coal."

The girl gasped. "Soft coal is the root of all evil."

"Love of money is the root of all evil. Don't you tree huggers read the Bible. Nothing in the Bible about soft coal and fracking, but it's real clear that you'll go straight to hell if you love money."

The girl's eyes hardened into little black marbles of disdain. She jumped off Roger's lap and turned to face him, fists on hips.

"Don't ever trash money to someone of my generation, you dip," she said. "I want a $5,000 wire transfer to my bank account on Christmas Eve or I will tell the kid who can ship you to Myanmar your real name. *Roger.*"

Roger grinned for the first time all afternoon. "That's more like it."

SUMMER 2020

The problem kicked off when Juniper Walsowski-Smith asked her grandmother Heather Heidi for $2,000 toward a certification in Forest Bathing.

Juniper was steeping fennel fronds in almost but not quite boiling water from Iceland, making a tea guaranteed to out-relax Xanax. She said, "I aspire to guide spirits into tranquility."

Heather Heidi tossed a bar of Dr. Bronner's Castile Soap at her granddaughter. "Bathe in the forest with this. Cuts down on toe jam and saves two thousand."

Juniper wouldn't touch the Castile. It was too harsh even for her fingertips. "We bathe ethereal cores in the forest, grandma. Tree bark invigorates chi."

Heather Heidi opened the refrigerator and pulled out a Red Bull. "Is your chi naked when you wash it in the woods?"

"Some choose to Forest Bathe nude. Personally, I wear Stio."

Heather Heidi popped the top. "Last time I got naked in the woods I was your age. Came home with four ticks. Those buggers love damp and dark."

Juniper said, "*Ew*, Grandma. TMI."

Heather Heidi had no clue what TMI meant, so she plowed

on. "What's the difference between Forest Bathing and sitting on a rock next to babbling creek, besides $2,000?"

Juniper drew out the little wicker basket of fennel, leaving a lime Jello-looking liquid in the cup. "They're nothing alike. Sitting on a rock leads to daydreams. When done with purpose, Forest Bathing blossoms into mindfulness."

"That's my second least favorite word, after karma. Why can't you say, 'Pay attention?' I pay attention outdoors. Otherwise you step in a badger hole and break your ankle like your grandfather Clyde did in college when he went Forest Pot Smoking."

Juniper sipped her tea, made a wrinkly face, and stirred in two tablespoons of locally harvested honey. "Mindfulness is absorbing your surroundings, soaking the very substance of the world into your blood. You never soak nature into your blood. You hike."

"Okay, smarty-shorts, which needle makes better floss — spruce or fir?"

"Those are trees?"

"You spirit guide can't tell a lodgepole from a totem pole."

"She concentrates on audio and odor, not artificial labels."

"Can she smell the difference between bear and coyote poop? I can. I can tell you the gender of an elk at a hundred yards without seeing it."

On this last rant, Clyde wandered into the kitchen, searching for food. He said, "Black bear poop has berries. Grizzly poop has tiny bells."

Juniper ignored him. "I also need a trip to Japan. The authentic bathing forests are in Japan. That's where haiku comes from."

Clyde said, "There's a national forest out the back door. You can stay home and still win the first place trophy."

Now, he'd hit on the current family sort spot. Juniper almost raised her voice, but, of course, she didn't. "Forest Bathing is not competitive."

Clyde stole Heather Heidi's Red Bull. Couples who have been together fifty years do that sort of thing, especially if the one doing the stealing is male.

"Nonsense," Clyde said. "Everything in America is competitive."

Clyde's been taking a load of grief from his loved ones of late for signing up for a hiking contest. The winner has to hike every mapped trail in Grand Teton and Yellowstone, stopping for a selfie once a mile for authentication. All of it ends up on Instagram.

Competition hiking gets Heather Heidi so incensed for the moment she forgot the Forest Bath.

"Walking in the mountains is the human way to touch God," she said. "It's spiritual. It's not how we win a medal."

Clyde chugged Red Bull. "At least I smell the rosehips. Randy Anders speed climbs. Fastest one from the car to the peak and back wins. He doesn't even pretend to see nature."

Heather Heidi made a *Tut* sound. "That's obscene. Some things should be done for inner grace. Not to beat your peers."

Clyde either laughed or smirked. With him, it can be a trick to tell which is which. "There is no point in an action if you can't win at it."

"Fly fishing?"

"There's folks making thousands of dollars catching and releasing fish, although trout pay a lot less than bass."

Juniper said, "Mandy Jane is in Santa Barbara at a yoga meet right now. She aspires to be a master yogini."

As usual, Heather Heidi was outraged. "Yoga is a practice, not a game. Competing goes against the whole spirit of being spiritual. It should be no more scored than singing in the shower or a detox body cleanse."

"I'll bet dollars to donuts there's a detox circuit," Clyde said.

"They'll start meditation next."

"That's already a sport," Juniper said. I'm thinking to try out."

"Meditation as sport?"

"They have one-on-one single elimination tournaments. March Mindfulness. The athletes wear brain sensing headbands that pick up EEG. You get five minutes and the one whose machine registers the blankest is declared Mellowest Dude."

Heather Heidi opened the refrigerator for another Red Bull. She protected this with both hands. "A prize for not thinking. Clyde would win that in a heartbeat."

Clyde jumped on his phone to Google *Things that shouldn't be competitive but are.*

"Here's a Bible verse contest series. This one I'm reading about second place shot the winner."

Juniper tossed her green tea down the garbage disposal and went for her own Red Bull. "I read about that. He said the winner cheated on Leviticus. Used an Alexa earpiece."

"Here's one that'll set your receptors tingling," Clyde said. "The Air Sex National Championship in Austin, Texas."

Heather Heidi put her imagination at play, but failed.

"How?"

"Like Air Guitar, only . . ."

"I don't want to know."

"Says here Austin is the Air Sex capital of America."

"Won't the girls in Wilson be jealous."

"Only rules are no nudity and you must have an imaginary person or object."

Juniper wrinkled her nose. "Object?"

"And no real orgasms."

Heather Heidi said, "How can they tell the difference. You never do."

WINTER 2020

March 1, 2024

As fate would have it, my PaPaw's 70th birthday and the end of our 48th month in isolation fell on the same day. To celebrate, my son Chub, who is stuck in an employee dorm at Old Faithful, set up a Zoom party for the family. Four years into this plague and I still haven't figured out Zoom. I can join meetings, but can't organize one.

So the three generations—PaPaw and MeMaw from their place in Moose, me (Peter Pym) and my wife Delores from our house in Jackson, our daughter Cora Ann in an apartment in Florence, Italy, where she is supposed to be studying Art History but isn't, and Chub—all got together on our various computer screens, looking like the opening credits from *Brady Bunch,* to sing "Happy Birthday" PaPaw.

I'm not certain he noticed. PaPaw has sort of faded in the last few years of sitting in his Barca Lounger, eating cheddar popcorn and watching TV.

The first year it was 1960s bowling, the so-called Golden

Age of Bowling. He was sharp enough to tell you Bill Bunette's average score on the pro circuit, but not sharp enough to distinguish Coke from Mountain Dew.

Then he discovered Willow TV—all cricket all the time. With no clue as to rules or terminology, PaPaw sat through 24 hours a day of boys in white flannels with little canoe paddles running from stick to stick. Every four hours or so they broke for tea. That's when PaPaw microwaved his popcorn.

PaPaw hasn't had a haircut since the original outbreak. He looks like Mr. Natural in his gnome phase.

"What's Dad watching these days?" I asked MeMaw, who has developed a weird eye tic. PaPaw doesn't seem to blink at all. MeMaw's eyelashes flutter like a moth caught in a sticky trap.

"He's stuck on Dog TV," she said.

Delores asked, "Is that like Pet TV only more niche?"

MeMaw fluttered. "Pet TV is for people who own pets. Dog TV is for dogs. You work at home and feel guilt about not playing with your dogs, you plop them in front of Dog TV all day. It's mostly Frisbee catching or sleeping by the fireplace."

I found this intriguing. "And PaPaw watches with Ski-Daddle?"

"Ski-saddle can't watch. Our TV isn't digital. Dogs can't focus on the picture on pre-digital televisions."

I didn't know that. Even in lock-up, you can learn new things.

MeMaw fluttered onward. "They did a study and dogs get nervous when TVs bark, so the videos run with light classical music and no dog sounds. I think PaPaw likes the music better than the Stupid Dog Tricks, but it distracts me from my puzzles."

MeMaw has dedicated her self-quarantine to jigsaw puzzles. She orders 1,000-piece boxes from Puzzle Overstock.

"The last one was all lavender and took two months. I'm running out of space," MeMaw said.

Mom can't stand the thought of breaking up a masterpiece so the leaves them where they are and orders a new card table from Amazon. My parents have 17 set-up card tables in their house now, each one sporting its own table-sized work of jigsaw art.

"My new puzzle is the Tetons from Shadow Mountain," MeMaw said. "You'd be surprised how many puzzles make use of Teton shots. They have the aspens in autumn. Makes it almost impossible to tell pieces apart."

"I have a continuous loop of the Dornan's webcam," Cora Ann said. "I rode my bicycle toward the Cathedral Group for nine and a half hours yesterday while listening to Hidden Falls. Then I counted cats out my window. I'm up to 5,281, although some might be repeats."

"Were you wearing hazmat?" I asked, feeling like I was addressing Charo on Hollywood Squares. Cora Ann's wardrobe has morphed to designer hazmat. Technically, she could go outside in Italy if she borrowed a dog to walk, but she doesn't. Instead, she drinks chianti and rides her stationary bike into a nature scene.

"Of course." She did a little twirl in front of her computer camera. "This one is by Alberta Ferratti."

Her suit was stylish. It had the Ferratti logo—a Chinese word looking ink spot—across the mask and fake prison tattoos running up the sleeves. I suspect Cora Ann sleeps in hazmat. I'm afraid to ask.

Delores, my lovely wife, reads the news off her phone from get-up to go-to-bed. She's obsessed with infection rates and hotspot curves. In between news flashes she writes letters-to-the-editor.

Chub asked if there are any editors left since the Emperor closed all media.

"They call themselves Influencers now," Delores said. "They keep popping up on blogs and vlogs. Bogs, all kinds of new places. The Emperor is playing Whack-A-Mole." A lot of them come out of Delaware since Delaware broke off into their own nation.

Teton County tried to form a break-away but the government sent in mercenaries from Ottawa and that's why we haven't been outside, officially, in two years. I sneak out at night to collect feathers and road-kill hide for my fly tying. That's what I do to pass time. I tie flies.

My flies keep getting bigger as the months go by. I've created flies big as bats. They scare Delores when I leave one in the bed.

Chub was at Old Faithful on a school field trip when the Wichita, Kansas, riots broke out and everyone was ordered to shelter in place for life. He watches the geyser go off from his window. The Park employees have a group competition for who can watch every episode of every show on Netflix.

Chub was leading till he got to "Umbrella Academy," which gave him an eating disorder that made pizza smell like West Thumb.

The competition winner receives a rock Cornish game hen that popped out of Teton Glacier during the Great Melt of 2022. Chub has a girlfriend he's never seen in West Covina, California, although I suspect she's a Russian bot. So many Californians are.

So, we sang "Happy Birthday" to PaPaw while he watched a dachshund ride a mechanical vacuum cleaner around a nursing home. MeMaw showed us a completed jigsaw, which was a photo of the last polar bear cut into a thousand pieces. Delores read us a letter-to-the-editor deploring the name change from Oklahoma to Trumpville. I showed them a dead hummingbird on a hook, Cora Ann saw a cat with two heads, and Chub stuck his phone to the window while Old Faithful soared skyward

A typical day for a typical family in 2024.

SUMMER 2021

The summer of 2020 brought a veritable swarm of tourists to Yellowstone, which would have made for a slow Grand Prix de Yellowstone except for the missing hazard — tour buses. Those lumbering cross between Triceratops and mud turtles were outlawed. Roads were wide open.

Or so thought Roger Ramsey, Clyde Walsowski-Smith, and the other race drivers. What they didn't realize was how many of the coastal refugees fleeing the plague were amateur tourists. On an average year, most of the tourists have been here before and know not to slap their kids on a buffalo's rump for a selfie uploaded straight to Instagram and the rescue helicopter.

They didn't know hotels, campgrounds, and toilets would be shut, the restaurants take-out only, and the bears aggressive. Last fall, after the summer rush, Wyoming changed its state flower to the used Pamper.

Which brings us to the Grand Prix de Yellowstone. Basically, it's one of those secrets that everyone knows, like Fox is to news what professional wrestling is to sports and the Golden Globes are rigged.

The rules: Vehicles tear out of Flagg Ranch at noon on July 2. They rip around the 142-mile double Yellowstone loop, stopping at Lake for tacky souvenirs, Mammoth for Rocky Road ice cream, and Old Faithful where you must witness an eruption and say something inane (Most drivers fall back on *"It used to be bigger.*).

Fifteen minutes are added if you receive a ticket, ten for running over an animal, and five for hitting a tourist. Five minutes are taken off for every sideswiped RV rearview mirror. Each driver has an observer on board to made certain the rules are followed and to open snacks.

That's where I came in. I was Braford Curtis's observer. Braford held the record for the only five-hour Yellowstone vacation in history, although there are rumors he skipped the upper loop to soak in the Firehole River.

Be that as it may, three cars, an SUV, and a pickup truck spun gravel at the stroke of noon — Clyde, Roger, Braford, Trixie Mudd with her sister Trippy, and my daughter Cora Ann with four gorpers I didn't know. Lynette Mosebee raced a Diamondback bicycle on the theory the rest of us would spend eight hours in a bear jam like what happened in 2019.

Braford took the lead by shooting through the Employees Only lane at the entrance station. Braford is a Park employee. Did I forget to mention that? Last summer he was head of mask enforcement.

At the north end of the Lewis River Canyon Braford stopped his Ford Bronco dead middle of the road, jumped out and ran to the canyon rim, pointing and hollering *"Griz!"*

Cars slammed brakes, both behind and coming toward us, doors flew open, binoculars, tripods, and IPhones sprouted like umbrellas at the beach. In five minutes we had traffic trapped for miles both ways.

That's when Braford strolled back to the Bronco and we drove off. He lit a cigarillo and grunted, "It'll take those jokers two hours to wade through that," and it did, all except Lynette who blew by us in the turn lane at Grant Village.

Braford said, "We'll lose her on Craig Pass."

At the Lake Hotel gift shop we passed over bamboo bison socks, ten dollar painted rocks, shellacked slabs of Douglas fir with pithy sayings about the weakness of males, elk poop earrings, and a set of whiskey glasses each with its own mountain range embedded in the bottom until we found the king of national park tacky — the *Tales of Yellowstone* vinyl album written and recorded by Kevin Costner. There really is such a thing. When I gave it to my wife she was floored.

At Mammoth Braford switched out his Rocky Road for a Sierra Nevada Pal Ale. When I threatened to report him, he bought me a shot of Grand Marnier to dribble over my ice cream.

Somewhere around the Madison River we came up on an EIEIO (Eastern Idaho Early Irons Organization) rally — antique car nuts who had to really stretch to come up with a flippant acronym. The antique cars topped out at twenty-five miles an hour. Many had those multi-tone European sirens with volume control instead of horns and when we blew by them on the shoulder they let loose with an *Aw-OOOO-Gah* that caused marmots to hibernate and moose to miscarry.

Braford waved and smiled.

As we swept onto the almost but not quite cloverleaf leading into Old Faithful, Braford tossed me his phone.

"Check out the app to see when she's blowing?"

"You have a geyser app?"

He nodded. "Got Old Faithful down to a thirty second gap.'"

I was dubious. "I don't think Old Faithful is that faithful."

Braford let out a snort. Picture an Irish wolf hound dry heaving grass. "Old Faithful's been plugged since the 2009 earthquake, but YP and the Park Service had so much invested in hotels and museums they've plumbed it. Old Faithful is no more natural than a hedge funders empathy."

That's when we ran over a Uinta ground squirrel, generally known as a chiseler.

"You just lost ten minutes," I said.

He downshifted with a jerk. "Squirrels are fake too. All the animals are artificial, and the trees and rocks. Nothing in Yellowstone Park is real anymore."

"Where'd you hear that?"

"On the QAnon web site, next to the *Cannibals of Beverly Hills* story. Amazon bought Yellowstone three years ago. They've stashed it in a Fulfillment Center outside Conroe, Texas. It's like *West World*. You ever see the TV show *West World*?"

"I don't watch TV," I said somewhat smugly.

"Everything is human designed, even most of the people here are brain scooped clones."

"How do you tell the real people from the clones?"

"The clones wear red hats."

At the geyser boardwalk Old Faithful gave some of those false starts amateur tourists waste film on while Braford explained to two guys from Australia about Amazon controlling nature.

"You should look in the hole and see the pipe," Braford said.

One Australian winked at the other. "We lie to tourists also. Every local the world over does."

"Go ahead and walk on out there and check out Old Faithful's gasket if you don't believe me."

So they did.

In the ensuing chaos Braford and I slipped off back to the Bronco.

Braford chortled. "We're going to beat five hours, easy."

And we would have set the new record if at the top of Craig Pass we hadn't been blocked by Cora Ann and her four gorpers who had joined an animal rights group to block the highway while a porcupine gave birth on the No Passing yellow stripe.

I got out and walked over to see how Cora Ann was doing. She sat, cross-legged, on the pavement, drinking this thing called a strawberry lemonade vodka slushie.

She said, "I wonder what it feels like to give birth to a porcupine? Wouldn't there be prickles?"

I said, "They're not real, you know. They're Amazon Prime."

"We know, but the animal rights people don't. They're naïve."

Braford came stomping up. "I'm gonna kill that porcupine."

Which leads to why we didn't break the five-hour Yellowstone vacation and why Braford had to Google *quill removal*.

HUFFINGTON POST CANADA

After Right Kind of Wrong, *based on* Sex and Sunsets, *by me, opened at the Toronto Film Festival, I was asked to write a blog in* Huffington Post Canada. *God knows why. I did that a couple times a week for maybe a year but then I ran out of gas and quit. Here is a sample of what I was doing. Mostly I stole old blogs and columns from myself.*

HUFF POST 1

W hen she was thirteen years old, Tanya Tucker had a big crossover country/pop hit called "Delta Dawn." Suddenly, in the blink of an eye, she found herself famous, the Miley Cyrus of her day. Tanya went into a wild spell marked by extremes, outrageous behavior, and public delamination of the celebrity sort. Now, she's grown into a respected icon of country music, which, goes to show you — survival is the most important element in becoming an icon. You, too, can become a venerated elder of your tribe, no matter what you did as a teenager. It's a matter of not stopping till you get there.

Anyway, Tanya Tucker put together an anthology called *100 Ways to Beat the Blues*. In the book, 100 more or less well-known people talk about their personal remedies for fighting depression. Mostly, she chose country singers and movie stars, along with a smattering of politicians and sports guys. And me. Lord knows how I made the cut. I've never met Tanya, although I have enjoyed her music and she seems to have come through the too-young fame syndrome with some level of sanity.

There are a few writers in the 100— Wally Lamb, Kinky Friedman, Cathie Pelletier. Not many live west of Austin. George And Barbara Bush had to share a chapter. Willie

Nelson's advice is short — "If you don't like the blues, play from the whites." I'm thinking it's a golf joke. Garth Brooks chapter is serious, sincere, and personal. Among other things, Garth says you should watch the news on TV every night. Whatever makes you happy, I guess. Roseanne said it's uplifting to beat the tar out of your ex-husband's motorcycle with a baseball bat.

An alarming number of the musicians recommend getting drunk. Personally, I found myself drunk a lot, back in the old days, and I don't remember it ever making me perky, punctual, and positive.

A bunch of the your more artistic types say depression is not necessarily bad for you.

Here is my chapter:

Kurt Vonnegut says a person must be depressed to write a novel, which is probably true. However, when I am depressed I have a tendency to sit on the couch and stare at that four-inch gap between my feet for several days, until the spiritual catatonia grows boring and I get up.

Boredom is the cure for long-term depression, and anything that alleviates boredom short-term — alcohol, sex with people you don't like, rage — only puts off the cure. So, after a few days of sitting there like an African violet in need of sunlight, I get up and fix a pot of Kenya AA coffee. Then I pop *Shane* into the DVD player. It's a scientific fact that a person cannot remain in the dumps throughout a full viewing of *Shane*.

Alan Ladd, Jean Arthur. Jack Palance.

"Shane! Come back! Mother wants you!"

The movie will renew your faith in the inevitability of good's victory over evil, the dignity of beauty, and the inspiration brought on by a nice view.

After *Shane*, and a couple of cups of strong Kenya AA, I can return to my work, refreshed and ready to produce.

That riff is the closest I've come to a bestseller.

I once saw Tanya Tucker at the Cowboy Bar. She was with Glen Campbell, at the height of her public flame-out. Lindsay Lohan and Britney Spears are flashes in the pan compared to a country singer gone off the steep side of the roller coaster. Tonya had taken some sort of strange pills and got herself stuck up against a wall in the Cowboy Bar ladies room. Folks went in and out of there for a couple hours, trying to peel her loose.

Then, suddenly, Tanya bounced on stage, grabbed the microphone, and belted out one of the most kick-ass sets I've ever seen or heard. She was a true professional, and a hot singer. I later used that scene in Western Swing. Nothing is wasted.

HUFF POST 2

I would like to be remembered as the man who invented the word gazillion. Not that I did, but most people given credit for creating things didn't. I would encourage you to tell your friends that Tim Sandlin coined the gazillion.

Which isn't what this blog is about. This blog is about human evolution.

On our way to Yellowstone the other day we came upon a major bear jam up around Pacific Creek. A couple hundred cars were pulled over and the display of photo equipment was truly impressive. There were lenses the size of bazookas aimed at this mother grizzly and three cubs that appeared to be grazing out in the field. I know, you are thinking grizzlies don't graze, but it sure looked like they were eating grass. Maybe it was for the same reason my dog eats grass — so they could crap indoors.

Anyway, the token idiot from Utah wandered out in the field for a close-up. Suddenly, the interesting nature lesson became one of those Darwin Award deals. All the hundreds of thousands of dollars of equipment left the bears and moved to the idiot. I blame YouTube. And those TV shows of Stupid

Human Tricks, or Nature Gone Wild. Any tech weenie with a cell phone can get rich selling tragedy to network news now, so nature itself takes a backseat to the chance to make a buck.

People were saying, "God, I hope she just rips his arms off instead of killing him outright. It'll make for much better footage."

I told my daughter the man was committing suicide and we might be able to watch. All these comments about his brainless, stupid, Utah-like behavior were made within hearing distance of the man's wife and kids. After a bit, the woman herded her children back into one of those pickup trucks so big it takes six tires instead of four to keep them on the road. And the cab is big as a limo. They idle loud as an airplane. The boy was playing some kind of handheld game where he got to kill people, which is modern life for you. Kids are more interested in wasting electronic humans than watching their dad buy it from a grizzly bear.

The bear stood on her hind legs and looked at the guy, but she never charged. The crowd was disappointed.

She did pick off a jogger a week later. Bit him in the ear and shoulder. People who live in grizzly country don't call it jogging. We call it trolling.

A photographer in Yellowstone was mauled the same day as our near but not quite adventure with the idiot. The guy in Yellowstone was two miles from a trail and three from a road. The bear ripped out his eye, and the guy walked three miles with his eyeball hanging off the side of his face. I think. The news story said the bear ripped out his eye, and another story said doctors spent so-many hours putting his eye back in, which means he either carried his eyeball in his hand for three miles or it was hanging by mucus or whatever off his cheek there. Both make an interesting image.

I wonder if he could see out of it. I read that Frenchmen who were guillotined were able to see for around three minutes after their head popped off their body. I don't know how the scientist who figured this out figured it out, but I suppose it's possible. The eye and the brain are both there together. You could see until oxygen became a problem. It would be fun to write a poem under those conditions.

HUFF POST 3

Throughout the 1970s and into the early 80s, I spent my summers and falls living outdoors, illegally, on National Forest land. The first few years, I lived in a tent, then later a homemade Cheyenne tipi. Nowadays, what we did is called homelessness. Back then, it was living in the woods. Millions of tourists paid big money to sleep outside like me. The only difference I could see was they had an indoor bed (and bathroom) to go back to.

The plan was to make enough money to move to town for the winter. Come September and October I found a job with a guaranteed lay-off so I could claim unemployment for six months and write a book. I wrote four unpublished and unpublishable novels this way, until the breakthrough in 1987. I turned 35 living alone in a backpacking tent up on Crystal Creek, reading Saul Bellow by flashlight light.

There were two years — '77 and '78, as I recall — where the only work I could find in the fall in Wyoming was in big game processing. I became an elk skinner. I had to wear a hairnet and a hard hat. The hairnet was because I hadn't cut my hair in a dozen years and the boss was a redneck. The hard hat was because the elk hang on meat hooks that could cold cock your ass if you didn't watch where you were going.

I wore a chain link belt with two knife sheaves and a slot for my sharpening steel. Big Mickey Mouse boots. We had a large barrel where all the bones and scraps and cigarette butts and the occasional Coke can went for the animal byproducts man to pick up every Friday. To this day, I can't eat anything that lists byproducts as an ingredient. Can't even feed the stuff to my dog. People speak admiringly of Indians who used every bit of a buffalo when they killed it, but those Indians were wastrels compared to the modern meat industry. Indians didn't use the glop found inside the lower intestines.

Deer and antelope are easy to skin. They peel like a banana. Elk and moose are harder because the muscles are attached to the hide, which is why they can do that skin flicking maneuver to shake off flies. I don't recall skinning a buffalo. There weren't that many around back then. I did sleep under a buffalo robe for a few winters. They aren't like blankets. As your body heat warms the hide, it forms a soft shell around your body, like a leather glove. Or a warm tortilla. Quite comfortable, especially if you can ignore the tiny bugs in the hair.

I only skinned one bear. Most hunters kill bears for the hide and head instead of the meat. They think a nice bearskin rug in front of a crackling fire will make them irresistible to women. Here's advice to those of you who would like to get laid on a bearskin. Make sure you're the one on top. Hollow bear hairs up your butt are not conducive to romance.

Skinned bears give me and lots of other people the heebie-jeebies. A skinned bear looks remarkably like a child, say, ten years old, dipped in candle wax. A child with a slightly humped back and no head. It's the fingers, I think, that make them so disturbing. A skinned bear's hands and feet could pass for human, except the feet are on backwards. The big toe is on the outside. Personally, I could live the rest of my life in peace without ever skinning another bear.

I say I took the job out of a lack of any other work in Wyoming in the off-season, but the truth is I became an elk skinner because I thought it would look cool on a book jacket. Ten years before my first publication, I was already aware of marketing. It's the same reason I worked trail inventory for the Forest Service, buffed belt buckles, and sold Popsicles out of a truck that played insane music from loud speakers mounted on the roof, but not the same reason I became a cook at the Lame Duck. I went into egg rolls from desperation as opposed to publicity.

ABOUT THE AUTHOR

Tim Sandlin first came to Jackson Hole in 1959 when his father started working seasonally for Grand Teton Park. Tim became a permanent resident in 1973. He tells people he worked 40 entry level jobs in the valley but the truth is he lost count in the upper-20s. His resumé does include elk skinner, buckle buffer, trail inventory hiker, gardener for the Rockefellers, dishwasher at Anthony's and long-time egg roll roller at the Lame Duck. He has published ten novels and another book of columns. He wrote three screenplays that were produced as movies. He lives with his family in Jackson.

www.ingramcontent.com/pod-product-compliance
Lightning Source LLC
Chambersburg PA
CBHW060430180626
46817CB00007B/2749